BEWITCHING
the
GHOST

SODASAC PRESS
PUBLISHING HOUSE

Sodasac Press supports copyright. Copyright promotes creativity and free speech, and keeps the author well-stocked in coffee. Thank you for buying an authorized edition of this book. If this work was obtained from a pirate, please support the artist by purchasing a real copy. The only pirates we tolerate wear billowy shirts, thigh-high boots, and probably sing songs by Gilbert and Sullivan. No part of this book may be reproduced in any form or by any electronic or mechanical means, including information storage and retrieval systems, without written permission from the author, except for the use of brief quotations in a book review.

FIRST EDITION

Library of Congress Cataloging-in-Publication Data has been applied for.

For my Little Woman
You are astonishing

"I'M SO GLAD I LIVE IN A WORLD WHERE THERE ARE OCTOBERS."

-L.M. Montgomery

Chapter One

THE MEET SPOOK

C ontrary to popular belief, witches can't usually see ghosts. Just imagine if they could. They'd never get anything done.

Or take showers, for Merlin's sake.

There are exceptions, however, if you recall the infamous tale of Betty Barmichael, a most persistent ghost who made herself a great nuisance in the town of Crescent

Hollow. Of course, she was a witch herself—if only a mediocre one. But, as the story goes, she was quite put out when they served deviled eggs at her wake. So she haunted her coven sisters for making the atrocious things, the town egg farmer for having the audacity to own chickens, and the grocery store for selling the eggs and Miracle Whip. Everyone in the town's witch community agreed it was the Miracle Whip that put her over the edge. In the end, she was cast out by a simple apology incantation and a promise to bake fresh rosemary bread on the anniversary of her death for the next seven years.

Then there were the few months that Silas Jones, when he was a teenager, claimed he could "see dead people." Coincidentally, he got straight A's on all his warlock tests that semester, which was not normal for him. So, it would seem it all worked out in his favor.

But in general, one can still say that apparitions from beyond the veil are as common as getting struck by lightning under a full, strawberry moon.

Willow Ravensong would have been perfectly content to keep it that way. She didn't care much for magic or divination, spells or sigil work. In fact, she was exceedingly lousy at everything witchy. She wasn't like her mother or two sisters, who seemed to excel at it all.

Her mother, Esme, candle shop owner, purveyor of magical herbs and spices, and dealer of potions witches would line around the block for was practically a legend in Crescent Hollow. Her sister, Bliss, who, with the goldenest of golden locks, could charm any warlock into gifting her gemstone jewelry (or, from that one guy—a convertible Audi S5 with red leather seats). And her other sister, Ivy, a stunning beauty with jet black hair and magical prowess dripping from her perfectly polished fingertips. She was aloof and poised, the very picture of elegance.

The Ravensong women were all celebrated among wizardkind in the small town of Crescent Hollow. All except Willow. She was so well known for her blunders, witches would give her a wide berth when passing her on the street for fear of residual bad luck, or getting their eyebrows singed off.

"Really," thought Willow whenever this happened, "it was only that *one* time. And they grew back."

Nevertheless, she did come from pedigree wizard heritage, which was probably why she wasn't shunned altogether. Still, she would have given anything to leave it all behind. To do something mundane with her life, like those girls on the TV shows she liked, where their biggest problems were love triangles or money woes.

Those girls seemed to drink a lot of coffee, eat nothing but pizza, and spend their time reading classic (non-magical) literature.

She'd infinitely preferred to read about rakish men in waistcoats and cravats and women in empire gowns with genteel manners than even look at another grimoire.

She once read a book about a young woman who owned a bookshop and fell in love with the local weirdo with dark hair that would swoop over his forehead in the most disheveled and beautiful way. They would leave fun

3

notes in all the books and go on scavenger hunts. That sounded nice to Willow.

So it seemed almost serendipitous when a real estate listing for a little storefront in the town of Mysthaven came across her lap—and even better, it was just within her budget.

She decided, after the third time she saw the flier, that it must have been fate. Even though she was more of scientific mind—incidentally frowned upon as a person of wizard blood.

Her real estate agent, Astrid, described the place as quaint with old town charm—which Willow later discovered meant creaky and in need of repairs. But it had good bones, and was situated across from town square, however small that was. Blink and you'd miss it.

The little property Willow now owned (the signing of the deed had been her biggest accomplishment so far) had been vacant for some time, but before that, it had been a sports bar. Before that, a record store. And originally, it was a saloon called Moonstone Spirits and Brew. Something about that name appealed to Willow, probably the nostalgia of it since she loved anything prior to the twentieth century. So, she adopted it in a way, giving her establishment the name Moonstone Spirits and Books. After all, there was no harm in serving libations for book buying customers.

Everything was falling into place rather nicely. Even Kyle, her contractor (a forty-something man with a penchant for flannel and backwards baseball hats), was quick with renovations.

He had a team of four men, and Zephyr, Willow's friendly Bombay cat, took to every one of them, winding between their legs, soliciting a scratch behind the ears when the men were on break. Most of the workers obliged, and Willow thought how nice it was to acquaint herself with fellow cat lovers.

But one of the men, a strikingly handsome guy with a handlebar mustache (probably one of those hipsters), only glared at the cat. And when Willow hazarded a reassuring smile his way, he scowled and walked away.

"Dog people," scoffed Willow with a derisive snort.

Or maybe he was allergic. She decided she'd give him the benefit of the doubt until she had more information.

But there was a strange pull she felt whenever he was present. The way her tummy swooped and the fine hair on her arms danced with static electricity. The way his biceps filled out the sleeves of his linen button-down shirt, and the way his dapper wool vest stretched across his torso with a single gold chain draping from the pocket. Certainly an unusual way to dress for someone installing bookshelves. But who was Willow to judge?

Her cheeks pinked the couple of times he caught her staring, the way he leaned against a wall with his arms crossed. The casual elegance. And oh, such soulful eyes—a luminescent green like the glass of a beer bottle held up against the sun.

He was simply the most attractive specimen of a man she'd ever seen. Too bad he was a sourpuss.

On the final day of renovations, when Willow was set to move into the small apartment above the shop, she made a point to bring home baked goods as her humble offering of gratitude for Kyle and his men.

Baking was the one thing she did well, as long as it didn't involve magic. Her mother's kitchen was hardly used for things like that. Esme was good with herbs and potions, but that was about as domestic as she got. Meals were almost always brought about by magic, and now Esme and Willow's two sisters would miss her browned butter snickerdoodle cookies and salted caramel apple tarts.

When Willow arrived at the shop, having an overly full bladder after a two-hour drive, she made a beeline for the ladies room. But there stood the green-eyed man, taking up the entire door frame that led to the back hallway where the restrooms were. Willow stopped abruptly in front of him, hoping he'd slide out of the way. But not only did he stay put, he glowered at her, tilting his head to the side like she was the oddest and most aggravating person he'd ever met and must be studied.

Fighting back a curse (and her bladder) Willow sucked in a breath and said, "Excuse me, please."

The man's eyes narrowed and a small twitch tugged at

one side of his mustache. But he didn't say anything. Or move out of the way.

Willow sighed, squeezing her Kegel muscles, willing herself not to pee her pants in front of this man. This infuriating and beautiful man.

"Look. I reeeeally have to go to the bathroom. Would you mind letting me pass? I brought cookies. Obviously I'm not taking the cookies into the bathroom. They're over there." She hooked her thumb over her shoulder in the direction of the bar. "Go ahead and take a tin home with you. I made a batch for everyone."

The man glanced briefly at the bar, then back at Willow, his eyes skating over her features, his lips parting ever so microscopically.

He was so attractive, she momentarily forgot all about having to take a wee.

Then, after a long pause, he pivoted his body, pressing his back against the threshold, and leaving a small space for Willow to pass.

What was with this guy?

Willow's current biological state didn't afford her the time to speculate. But as she slid by him, there wasn't the usual warmth one would expect from such close proximity to a man. Instead, she felt a coolness sweep over her, like the first day of autumn, or the chill one gets when drinking an iced beverage. Not entirely unpleasant, just surprising.

But the flame in her cheeks soon warmed her all over as her eyes snagged on his penetrating stare, and even as she walked down the hallway, feeling the weight of his gaze on her until she turned the corner, silently chastising herself for enjoying the encounter a little too much.

She really needed to work on her creep-o-meter.

When she finished her business, he was gone. *Thank the Graces.*

She spotted Kyle gathering up the last of his tools and wandered over to him.

"Everything looks great. Did all your workers go home already?"

She was trying to keep her curiosity in check. Was she being too obvious as she looked around to see where the green-eyed man had gone?

Kyle's eyes crinkled as he smiled at her. "Not much work to do today. Just some finishing touches."

"Do you think they'll be back?"

"Nope. Not unless you need something else done. If anything's not working properly, just give me a call. I guarantee all my work."

"Oh. Good to know."

Willow didn't quite know how to ask about the men, if they lived locally, or if one in particular had a stick up his trousers.

"I'll send the invoice to your email. Is that okay?"

"Great! Yes, that's fine. And please tell the guys thanks. They did an awesome job."

"That's why I hired them."

Kyle turned to leave but Willow called after him, thankfully remembering the tins of cookies on the bar.

"Wait. I almost forgot."

She ran back to the bar, gathering all five of the tins in her arms. Kyle, the gentleman that he was, rushed over to help her.

"What's this?" he asked.

"Cookies. Pumpkin chocolate chip, cinnamon rum balls, and chewy maple sugar. There's one tin for each of you. I was hoping to give them out myself, but if you could take them with you, I'm sure you'll see your men before I do."

"How kind. I'll definitely make sure they get them."

"And they really should be eaten fresh. So, if they have kids. Or wives..."

Willow cringed inwardly at herself. She might as well have held up a sign that read, *I'm single and super curious about that Dapper Dan with no trace of a wedding ring on his finger.*

Yes, she'd looked.

"A couple of my men have kids at home. I'm sure they'll appreciate the cookies."

Willow hoped the disappointment hadn't played on her features. After all, if the hipster guy was single, what would she even do about it?

He was rude. He was surly. And he probably vaped or something off-putting like that.

No thank you.

Kyle stacked four of the tins in one hand like it was nothing, nodding as he shuffled towards the door.

"Well, I better head out. I promised my kids I'd take them to the pumpkin patch."

"Sounds like fun. Oh, don't forget this one."

Willow held out the last cookie tin. Darn that vexatious man for leaving without it.

"I've got the four you gave me," said Kyle. "One for each man."

"Yes. One for each of the four workers, and one for you, too." She shook the tin at him.

Kyle ticked his head to the side. "I only have three men."

"I could have sworn I counted four," she said, puzzled.

In fact, she knew she had. How could she forget the attention they gave Zephyr? All except *him*.

Where *was* Zephyr, anyway?

"Nope. Just three."

A shiver snaked up Willow's spine. She'd heard about things like gaslighting, but had no reason to suspect her contractor would try to mess with her head like that.

"Three? But the guy that was just here..."

She proceeded to list them all off, just to be sure she wasn't going crazy, but Kyle stopped her before she could finish.

"What guy? I'm the only one that came today."

"The man with the mustache and green eyes."

"Not one of mine."

"But..."

"You know, Mysthaven is a relatively safe town. But

maybe you should invest in a double lock. I'll pick one up for you next time I'm at the hardware store."

"If he wasn't one of your men, who was he?"

He shook his head and seemed a little concerned, bless him. "I didn't see him, sorry. But I can check all the rooms before I go. Just to be safe."

"No, I'm okay."

Willow might have been a poor excuse for a witch, but she knew better than to mess with the protection enchantment Esme placed on her before she left home. It would last a few days, anyhow.

Just then they heard a crash from upstairs and Kyle quickly set down the cookies and ran to investigate. Willow followed behind him ready to be righteously pissed off at the hipster hottie, but when they entered her new bedroom, they only found Zephyr playing with a box he'd knocked over.

Willow was mortified for Kyle to see the contents spilled out on the floor. Still, he didn't say anything about the racy covers of her romance novels or the various witchy things her sisters must have slipped in there without her knowledge. She'd have a few words with them next time she saw them.

She scooped everything up while Kyle searched the whole upper floor and puzzled over when she'd brought that particular box upstairs.

It must have been on one of her previous trips.

"All clear," Kyle said, returning to the scene. "But a

security camera or two wouldn't be amiss. Better safe than sorry."

"Got it."

It was times like this she wished she knew a few blocking spells for the shop. Well, she *knew* some spells, but knowing something and not screwing them up were two different things entirely.

"Tomorrow," she thought. Tomorrow she'd get to know some of the locals and maybe find out who might be this mysterious stranger.

Then she'd go find him and kick him in the bean bags for hanging around a construction zone. What if he'd stepped on a nail and sued her?

But as providence would have it, she didn't need to search very far. And *that* turned out to be more disturbing than she'd bargained for.

"THE WITCH KNOWS
NOTHING IN THIS WORLD IS SUPERNATURAL.
IT IS ALL NATURAL."

-Laurie Cabot

Chapter Two

THINGS THAT GO BUMP

W illow Ravensong loved a good jump scare as much as the next witch, but on her first night away from the familiar and cozy surroundings of her childhood home, and away from her mother and sisters, she began to question the Wes Craven movie marathon.

Yes, this was the Ravensong women's Wednesday night tradition: spooky movies in bed, curling under the blankets with snacks, surrounded by pillows. And her cat at her feet, while her sisters snuggled next to her, casting 4-D enchantments over the TV so images and feely things would highlight the experience. Such good times.

She supposed, as she sat on her bed, she felt a pang of homesickness—tonight being the first time she'd ever been alone. And with the nostalgia of it all, what else should she have done with her Wednesday night?

But there was no 4-D enchantment. So what was that strange tickle up her spine and the odd sense of... something in the air?

In the twilight's waning embrace, amidst the quietude of the otherwise sleepy town, she clutched her popcorn and pressed pause on the remote, thinking she'd heard a noise. But it was just Zephyr breathing, fast asleep at the foot of the bed. That, at least, was familiar.

"I can do this," she said, thinking about how failing at this business venture was not an option. "It's a great opportunity."

If nothing else, she wanted to prove it to herself.

And even though the bookshop was her favorite part of the business, there was a quaint charm to the bar. Ah, that charming old thing that had the hallmarks of a Hallmark movie. By day, it was all smiles and rainbows, the kind of place a lovestruck hero might meet their match. Yet, come nighttime, it felt more like a set piece for a ghostly gala. No worries though—a sprinkle of bean bags and more fairy lights would do the trick.

And just in case, she'd call Kyle first thing in the

morning to install those cameras before the grand opening.

She unpaused the movie, comforted by a lone candle bravely battling the darkness, casting shadows that danced like drunken trolls on the walls. The air hung heavy, as if even the breeze had given up on its usual routines.

Then, a sudden chill permeated the room, causing the candle's flame to shiver and bend, and the window rattled with an abrupt thud.

Willow's head snapped up, her eyes darting outside. But beyond the window, the trees stood guard like bouncers guarding an enchanted nightclub, their branches having a serious conversation with the moonlight.

"Just a bit of wind's mischief," she quipped, though her heart was doing the cha-cha in her chest. "Or the building's way of saying, 'Hey, don't forget I'm ancient and quirky.'"

Undeterred, she huddled under her blankets and pressed her thumb on the remote, aiming to rejoin her movie marathon. Yet, during the movie's quieter scenes —when knives were taking a break from slashing bodies and bad guys were creepily watching the main characters sleep, Willow could almost swear she heard footsteps on the stairs, or the creak of a floorboard in the shop below.

With a dismissive shake of her head, she shrugged off the disquiet as mere figments of her imagination running amok, brought on by too much cheese with her dinner, or too much butter on her popcorn.

Clearly, dairy was in cahoots with her imagination. "No worries," she thought. "Things that go bump in the night just need flashlights."

With that thought, Willow clicked on the lamp by her bedside, blew out the candle, and shut off the TV for the night, choosing a book to help her drift into an easy slumber.

She dreamt of balls in grand houses, men in top hats, and carriage rides through the English countryside. When she woke the next morning, she imagined what it would be like to live in a time when women were courted by true gentlemen instead of the types of guys she knew back in Crescent Hollow who honked when they picked her up for dates. Or surly mustached hipsters with no manners or social skills to speak of.

"No way," she muttered to herself, putting her mental foot down against the intrusion of a certain green-eyed man who'd appeared, unbidden, in her thoughts. "Not on my watch."But the brewing storm of her imagination was soon usurped by another lively idea. "What if," she thought, "I throw a ball?"

Not just any ball, mind you, but one with Victorian opulence, where gowns swirled like autumn leaves and the air was thick with literary enchantment.

It would require quite a bit of planning which would take more time than she had before the grand opening, but a ball would be just the thing to create a buzz about the bookshop. The weekend before Halloween, she surmised, would be the perfect crescendo. What soul could resist the allure of dressing up?

As she imagined the fanciful details over her morning coffee, Kyle, who showed up ten minutes after she'd called him to install security cameras, met her at the bar.

"All systems go," he declared, dropping his toolkit with an air of accomplishment. "You'll be able to monitor every nook and cranny—except perhaps the restroom, for decency's sake. You want me to show you how to check the app on your phone?"

"I absolutely would," she said, smiling brightly. It was a wonder how a good idea like a ball could put her in such a great mood. "And while you're here, could you humor me and check the fuse box? It's not a huge deal, but the lights flicker every now and then. And this morning, my smart speaker was crossing signals with the international space station."

"Hmmm." Kyle looked up in thought as he rubbed his chin. "We replaced everything in the remodel. All new wiring, fuse box, light fixtures... which room is giving you trouble?"

"All of them."

"Okay, I'll take a look. We might have missed a connection." He shook his head, even as he walked away to wherever he needed to go to check on the electricity.

Then, as if the cosmos sensed an absence of lively company, in walked Astrid, a whirlwind of vivacity and curiosity.

"Hello, darling. I wanted to check up on how you're settling in and to give you some good news."

Astrid gave Willow two air kisses and looked around. "I love what you did with the place."

"Charming, isn't it?" Willow beamed, basking in Astrid's delighted observation. "I wanted to restore the original charm with some chic new accents. The chandelier looks old fashioned but it's new, and we used the same aesthetic of the bar for low bookshelves."

"Darling, you've done wonders," Astrid enthused. "Now, do you want to hear the good news? Of course you do. I pulled some strings with the powers that be. You know it pays to be universally liked in a small town like this."

Smiling smugly, she produced a stack of papers from seemingly out of nowhere. Was that tiny purse of hers like a Mary Poppins bag?

"Anyway, I've managed to resurrect the ancient liquor license through some, shall we say, persuasive dealings," Astrid revealed with a flourish, punctuating the statement with the suave extraction of a pen seemingly tailored for divine writing.

Willow, still on cloud nine from thinking about the ball she wanted to throw, simply blinked and grinned.

"I must say," said Willow, "I'm impressed. I was under the impression it would take months to get a license."

"Time is a mere trinket in the hands of the resourceful," Astrid declared, flicking her perfectly polished fingers in the air. "There are loopholes for everything, dearie. Sign here."

She tapped her nail on the contract marked with arrow stickers, and Willow, still caught in the undertow of her own tangled thoughts, signed the papers with all the enthusiasm of a squirrel discovering a hidden stash of acorns.

"Astounding," Willow marveled, even as her hand swooshed across the paper. "Months of bureaucratic muddling averted in a single flourish. I love this pen, by the way."

"Writes like a charm, doesn't it?" Astrid scooped up the papers and plucked the pen from Willow's fingers, not waiting for the ink to dry from the final signature. "Well, that's that. "Now, my dear, do you have your offerings in order for the grand opening?"

"Well, I probably should order more booze, now that I can sell it, thanks to you. I had this vision of pairing drinks with books, so whenever a customer picks something off the shelves, I'd suggest a cocktail to go with the theme."

"Oh that is a marvelous idea," said Astrid. "I love a good literary libation."

"Exactly. Like for instance, The Great Gatsby deserves to be matched with a Gin Rickey."

"Naturally."

"Whiskey daiquiri inspired by Hemmingway," Willow continued, pulling a glass from under the bar. "And I like to call this one Tequila Mockingbird. Hmmm."

"What is it, dear?" Astrid questioned, noting the look of confusion on Willow's face.

Willow scratched her head. "The tequila. I had it right here."

"You mean the bottle on the shelf behind you?"

Willow turned around, and sure enough, the bottle of tequila sat nicely on the shelf, the label lined up perfectly next to the other bottles—each of them in methodical order. Willow couldn't remember organizing them that way—especially considering she wasn't expecting to sell any alcohol for a few months yet. But she was tired from all the work she was doing. Work, not aided by magic in any way shape or form. So she must have forgotten what she'd already done.

"Yes. Silly me," she said, taking the bottle down. "Anyway, it's like a Bloody Mary with tequila instead of vodka. Would you like to try? It's basically a breakfast drink."

"Not on a Thursday. But I'll take a rain check on that. By the way, not to pry or anything, but have you hired help?"

Willow pulled a face. "I thought I'd take out an ad today."

"No need for that. A colleague of mine has a son who's looking for work. I'll send him your way."

"Uh... Thank you."

"Oh it's nothing. But I have to tell you... if you want to do business in this town, you absolutely must join the Mysthaven Women's Business Council. I simply cannot let another day go by without inviting you. We meet every other Tuesday morning. Seven A.M. sharp."

"Okay. Wow, that's early."

"Yes, well, we have to get started before businesses open for the day. We're all women entrepreneurs, you know. Rowena Crump owns a bakery and sometimes brings her pastries."

"Well, in that case..."

"I insist you come. No excuses. I'll text you the address. And to sweeten the deal, I'll make sure we have pumpkin spiced tea."

"Consider me there. Is there anything I can bring? Mimosas, perhaps?"

"I wouldn't hear of it. New members need not bring anything. Well, I must run. So much work to do before the weekend. Ta ta."

With a swish of her skirt and a flicker of her fingers, she exited through the front door with the same pizzazz as when she came in.

After a few minutes, Willow decided to go find Kyle to see if he found the electricity short.

"Kyle?" she called out, heading toward the storeroom. But as she turned down a hallway, she noticed a figure in the corner of her eye. Following the shadowy image, she caught a glimpse of the man with the mustache. He turned his head as he was walking by, pausing his stride to fix his gaze on her briefly, his green eyes shimmering with a curious expression.

"Hey. You can't be in here," Willow cried, and ran after

him. But he moved too quickly for her, and as she came upon the rear door that led to the alley, he was gone. With her heart pounding in her chest, Willow made sure to close the latch on the door as a chill swept over her, crawling up her spine and catching in her throat.

"WITCHES DON'T LOOK LIKE ANYTHING.
WITCHES ARE. WITCHES DO."

—Franny Billingsley

Chapter Three

MY MOTHER IS A FISH

The gift was a nice thought, as bookshop-warming gifts go, that is. And Esme was so proud for having brought it. But one would imagine a mother would know her daughter had a black thumb. So it would follow that she'd think twice before giving Willow a planter box full of herbs. But Willow didn't have the heart to tell her mother the plants would be dead within the week—even with Esme's magic surrounding them.

"Now you'll be able to serve the best mint juleps anyone has ever tasted," said Esme. "And I brought you sage because I know you love it."

"I do," said Willow, thinking about that orange-sage olive oil cake she made over the summer. Of course it was her mother's garden which supplied the herb, not her own attempt at husbandry. "I suppose I could add a blood orange sage martini to the menu. Or match Lord of the Rings with an elder sage cocktail."

"That's the spirit," said Esme, sipping on something with blueberries and gin. "This could use a sprig of rosemary."

And between the timespan of two blinks, a small stem of fresh rosemary appeared in her drink.

"You're welcome," said her sister Ivy with a twitch of her eyebrow. How Ivy did that eyebrow thing was a complete mystery to Willow. How she could conjure almost anything like that was beyond her understanding. Willow simply sighed because she knew better than to say anything to her sister for using magic in public. Ivy was a master at redirection, and even though it was the grand opening of Moonstone Spirits and Books, and the place was packed, not a single soul would notice the pocket of magic at their table. The only thing anyone would take a second glance at would be the seemingly unfair portion of beauty Willow's sisters were blessed with. And Esme, too, who was practically ageless. But it was Bliss who turned the most heads. If they made a witchy Barbie doll, it would look like Bliss.

"Thank you my love," said Esme. "Willow, take a mental note of this. Rosemary sprig. It makes all the difference in the world."

"I'll remember that," replied Willow.

"Did you unpack everything yet?" asked Bliss, looking like the cat that ate the canary.

"Yeah, that box of things was the gift that kept on giving. What did you cast on it? A bottomless pit spell?"

"It's just a simple dimensional charm," said Bliss, grinning. "Bigger on the inside."

"Yeah, sis. Thanks for packing my broomstick I'll never use. My contractor almost saw it fall out of the box. And the Witchcraft for Dummies book? Very funny."

Bliss snickered. "You love me."

"You're lucky I do, little sister."

One of Willow's joys in life was to remind Bliss of the sibling seniority she had over her, although there was only eleven months between them. And, being the middle child, Willow took what she could get in the hierarchy of her little family.

"We're all proud of you," said Esme, smiling warmly at Willow. One thing was for certain, she didn't have a favorite daughter, and was always sure to let the three girls know that. "And just to give me peace of mind, I placed a little protection enchantment over all the entryways. That Dapper Dan you told me about might be harmless, but we don't want to take any chances."

Dapper Dan. That was one way to describe him. Willow wasn't even sure she wanted to tell her mother about the mysterious intruder with striking green eyes, hipster vest, and a twirly mustache worthy of a silent film villain. After all, she wouldn't want Esme to worry. But Willow was never good at keeping secrets—especially from a woman as intuitive as Esme Ravensong. In the end, Willow didn't need to fret over it. Her mother was a practical woman, cool as a cucumber in the face of any potential threat. Nothing ever spooked her or alarmed her. She always took care of everything with composed alacrity. For Esme, something like a protection spell was akin to fastening one's seat belt, or using an umbrella in the rain.

"I do have locks on all the doors, you know," Willow reminded her mother. "And security cameras."

"That's cute, dear." Esme patted a dismissive hand over Willow's. "Now we must be off. Since you insisted we not use magic to get here, we have a two hour drive home."

Ivy threw Willow a pointed look, which was her way of telling her Esme was so full of it. They were definitely using magic to get home. Probably driving to Mysthaven's town limits and then using some kind of portal charm into Crescent Hollow. At least Esme was *trying* to humor her.

As soon as the three women left, the bustle of the bookshop flooded over Willow, as if a charm had been lifted, and the demands of the customers crashed around her like opening a closet door when everything was stuffed inside. But it was a good kind of busy.

Willow reveled in ringing up books and recommending cocktails. She'd even made book shaped sugar cookies for patrons to enjoy as they shopped, or read a little. Every corner of the store was humming with the excited chatter of her guests, and her heart warmed with gratitude toward the inhabitants of Mysthaven.

It wasn't until she'd taken a moment's reprieve that she noticed a lone figure through the crowd of browsing patrons. He was sitting in a wingback chair, legs crossed elegantly, and amusing himself with a book which sat open on an antique accent table. Willow figured he was too engrossed in the book to notice her approaching him, but when she was about three feet away, he gazed up at her, tilting his head ever so slightly. She was arrested by his look. Those impossibly green eyes with a trace of melancholy in them. And then there were the tiny hairs behind her neck which stood on end with the way he fixed his attention on her—cautiously and a little bit bothered.

Who was Willow to interrupt this man's reading? Only the owner of this fine establishment, that's who. He could at least buy something. Willow considered telling him so. But it was opening day. And there were a lot of people around. And Willow was anything but unpropitious.

She bent her head to get a gander at the book he was reading. *As I Lay Dying*. Kind of a morbid choice, but it was October, after all.

"Are you a fan of Faulkner?" she asked him as he watched her, unblinking. "Personally, I found the multiple narrators a bit jarring. Although I did enjoy the way he evokes mythical characters as a backdrop to the story. I actually had to read it twice to make sense of it. Is this your first time reading it?"

The man remained still, unmoving other than the parting of his lips—which Willow noted were nice-looking lips under the manscape of trimmed and tidy facial hair. And his skin. So white, it almost resembled a pearl.

"Can I interest you in a mint julep? That was Faulkner's favorite drink. I heard they're the best mint juleps anyone has ever tasted."

For a tiny moment, the man's eyes flickered, as if calculating his exit. But Willow was undeterred, and was determined to figure this guy out. Even though he seemed like he'd rather do anything than actually speak to her.

"I'm Willow, by the way. I... think we got off on the wrong foot the other day."

Willow enthusiastically offered her hand to the man, letting her arm hang between them, stiff as a board. He did not take her up on the handshake, only dropping his gaze to her outstretched hand and back up to her face.

"You're leaving me hanging here, man. Do you at least have a name?"

She awkwardly retreated her hand, suddenly not sure what to do with it. Letting it hang at her side felt too weird, now that this guy seemed to have an aversion to it... or normal greetings in general. Or maybe he was a germaphobe. She took a small step backwards just in case.

"Willow Ravensong, that is. I own this place. Gosh, it

feels strange to say that. '*I own this place*'. Gah! But I thought you should know that before you go thinking I'm some random lady asking men about Faulkner. Or what their name is. Or offering to buy them drinks. I'm not here fishing for phone numbers, or anything, that's all I'm saying."

Now would be a good time for her mouth to stop running.

The man had the expression of someone who either thought she was a nutcase, or didn't understand a word she was saying. But he was reading Faulkner. Surely he knew English.

He shifted his gaze to his right, followed by a slight turn of his head. Then to the left. He did it in the way one does when looking to see if anyone else was seeing this train wreck of a conversation, and if someone would please save him. Then he returned his cold stare at Willow, opened his mouth, and seemed to get his voice stuck in his throat before blinking, sucking in a breath as if it was demanding his entire concentration to do so, and in a dazed tone, said, "Mont... gomery. Har... land."

And then, as if shocked and delighted to remember how to talk, repeated himself.

"Montgomery Harland."

Willow smiled with a small sense of accomplishment.

"Nice to meet you, Montgomery Harland. I hope you find what you're looking for. Classics are fifty percent off today if you decide Faulkner's your jam."

She wanted to add 'but you're only welcome here

when we're actually open' but thought better of it and pressed her lips together.

The man stared at her incredulously and she thought of saying something witty or perhaps a joke about Proust, when someone's screaming child momentarily caught her attention. She only turned her head for a second or two. But when she snapped it back to Montgomery, he was gone.

"THE UNDISCOVERE'D COUNTRY,
FROM WHOSE BOURN
NO TRAVELLER RETURNS."

-William Shakespeare

Chapter Four

WEIRD GLOWS GLEAM

Broomsticks. What a cliché. Even though they were a cliche for a reason. Unfortunately, Willow never got the hang of it, no matter how hard Esme tried to coach her. Truth be told, she just plain hated it. Major chafing, and all that.

But her bike. That she loved. She could ride her bicycle 'til the cows came home. If she had nowhere to be, going around in circles suited her just fine. She could do a loop of the whole town in the same time it took to listen to *Strange Magic* by Electric Light Orchestra.

Today, she'd already gone to the florist for no other reason than to ride through town with a basket full of flowers.

The Mysthaven Women's Business Council wasn't held at the civic center like Willow would have imagined, but in a Victorian Stick style house on the outskirts of town. It stood three stories tall, with prominent eaves, a Queen Anne-style wraparound porch and a Gothic mansard roof.

Tucked away behind rows of silver maple, the grand old house sat at the end of a long driveway, and the sprawling backyard hugged the edges of the serene Cinnamon Woods, which were currently displaying the breathtaking reds, yellows and rust of autumn.

Until now, Willow didn't know she'd had a dream house, but if she did, this would be it. It was painted a soft gray with white trim, and with pumpkins practically spilling from the front steps, the cozy factor increased tenfold.

"Whoever lives here," she thought, while rolling her bike past no less than two parked Mercedes, "must be totally loaded."

Then, stepping onto the porch, she noticed the bespoke wooden sign hanging from two hooks that read '*The Law Offices of Bickford, Gluntz, and Pate.*'

Well, that explained a lot.

She didn't have to knock. Astrid herself flung open the door before Willow had a chance to raise her knuckles.

"Darling!" said Astrid, "You're right on time."

"Oh good," Willow replied, slipping out of her coat as she passed the threshold. "I don't know what came over me this morning, but I woke up at dawn feeling so refreshed, I was able to get all sorts of stuff done before coming here. Wow, your house is gorgeous."

"Oh, it's not my house, dear," said Astrid, leading her down a hallway. "This is Nadine Bickford's house. This is where she runs her law practice, and it's so quaint, the Women's Business Council decided to hold our meetings here whether she likes it or not."

Astrid snickers at her own words, like it was some kind of inside joke with the other ladies Willow had yet to meet.

"Well, I don't blame you," she replied.

Astrid paused at the end of the hallway, just outside a pair of double doors and turned to smile at Willow. Her teeth were perfect. Her red lipstick, flawless.

"I think you'll fit in just fine," she said, and opened the double doors to a sitting room so opulent, Willow wasn't sure if she should curtsey or bow.

There sat three other women, each one with poise and class up the wazoo. They were all in stylish business wear, but somehow the clothes draped over their slender figures as though they were Paris fashion influencers. Even lounging they looked super ritzy, crossing their legs at the ankles and all that.

Willow held back in the doorway for just a moment as she took in the sight, feeling monstrously underdressed.

"You must be Willow," said a woman with fierce cheekbones. "Welcome to my simple little haven."

"Hi." Willow waved dorkily. Lovely. If her mom jeans didn't scream, "Look at me, I'm a hillbilly ragamuffin," her manners certainly did.

"Nadine Bickford at your service. This is Rowena Crump, Daria Morgenstern, Jewels Duffy, and you already know Astrid."

"Nice to meet you all," said Willow.

"Rowena owns the bakery I told you about," Astrid said, ushering Willow to a high-backed chair.

This brightened Willow's mood considerably.

"Yes I do," Rowena said. "You must try the caramel turnovers."

"I'll get her one," said Astrid, already fluttering over to the sideboard. "Sugar in your tea, Willow?"

"Um, no thank you."

Willow wiggled in her seat, somewhat uncomfortable as the subject of every one of the women's curious stares. Her eyes darted from one to another, an awkward smile on her face, as they looked at her without a word.

The silence was finally broken by Astrid, bearing a plate with the caramel turnover and a cup of tea.

"Here you are," she sing-songed. "I admire a woman who takes her tea with no sugar. It's a sign of... maturity, I think."

"Oh yes," Nadine agreed. "So lady-like."

The woman who was introduced as Daria nodded primly, her black, bobbed curls bouncing with her head. "Indeed."

Jewels also nodded and muttered "Yes, yes, I'm with you on that one," and on and on.

Willow supposed the other ladies were going out of their way to make her feel welcome—they obviously were super successful business women. Astrid, being a big shot real estate girl boss, Nadine, with this enormous house and at least one of the Mercedes out front belonging to her, and a lawyer to boot.

What the other women did was a mystery to her, but judging by the finery they wore, she was certain they were doing pretty well for themselves.

And then there was her—who only was able to open Moonstone Spirits and Books due to a fluke of a property listing and a very motivated seller. Willow was truly lucky to have found it, and in turn, Astrid, who made the transition effortless.

"So," began Nadine, after a sip of her tea. "You've taken over the old saloon on the corner. We were all so thrilled to see a business open there. It's been vacant for ages. Congratulations."

"Thank you. I can hardly believe it myself."

"I heard you transformed it into a bookstore?" Jewels asked. "What kinds of books do you sell?"

"All kinds of books," Willow answered. "Old, new, romance, non-fiction. You name it."

"How marvelous," Daria chimed in. "I would love to

pop in sometime to peruse your history section. I'm just fascinated how ancient civilizations approached healthcare."

"Daria is a holistic medical practitioner," Astrid explained.

"The best there is," declared Jewels.

Daria flapped her hand, "Oh stop. But if you ever want to come to my office for a free evaluation, Willow, I'll give you the royal treatment."

"Thank you, that's very kind."

"You're one of us, now. We women entrepreneurs have to stick together."

The idea itself warmed Willow's heart, but as she looked around the room, she had to admit she was a little disappointed about the turnout. She wasn't sure what she'd expected at this meeting, but she at least thought there would be more women entrepreneurs present. Were there really only five female business owners in the entire town of Mysthaven?

She took a bite of her turnover and about died, it was so good. She must have groaned a little too audibly, because Rowena grinned proudly.

"Delicious, aren't they? Old family recipe I keep under lock and key."

Willow took another bite, the flaky pastry melting in her mouth. "Mmmm. Amazing."

Astrid clapped her hands. "It's time we get the meeting started, ladies. Willow, you happen to have stumbled upon us right in the middle of planning the

Mysthaven Harvest Festival. It falls on us every year."

"Oh that sounds like fun," Willow said.

"Except that one year," Jewels said. "Remember when Bo Richter took over the planning?"

"What a disaster that was," said Nadine.

"But we sure took care of him," Daria exclaimed.

Willow stopped mid-bite. "Took care of him?"

"It," said Daria. "I meant to say... we took care of *it*."

"Jewels swooped in to save the day," added Nadine.

Jewels was beautiful, and just as classy as the other ladies, but there was something of a bohemian air about her. Perhaps it was the print of her dress, or the crystal pendant. Or, as Willow was just noticing, Jewels was the only one of the women with bare feet.

"Go girl power," Willow said, pumping her fist in the air, like she was one of the Power Puff Girls. She quickly sank down in her chair. Fortunately, not one of the women reacted negatively.

Nadine cleared her throat and addressed Willow directly. "The Mysthaven business owners all take part by hosting some sort of booth. There are games and Halloween themed activities like bobbing for apples."

"I do the dead ringer ring toss," Jewels said. "That's always a hit with the teenagers."

"And I sell meat pies," Daria added.

"Oh!" exclaimed Willow. "I could bake cookies. I have a fab recipe for—"

"I make the cookies," said Rowena a little too snappy, but then brought it in after realizing her overreaction.

"Um, I meant to say that the townsfolk of Mysthaven look forward to my cookies every year."

"Oh, of course," said Willow, feeling silly. "I wasn't thinking."

"No troubles, dear," said Astrid. "Besides, we have something in mind for you. Our beloved Lola used to run the fortune telling booth, but sadly, she's no longer with us."

"I'm so sorry," said Willow completely sincere in her condolences, although she always thought she said the wrong thing in these situations. "When did she die?"

"Die?" Nadine cackled. "She didn't die. Lola moved to Florida."

Now Willow really felt like a dork. Why was she this way?

Astrid gestured to Daria who dug inside her extra-large bag and produced a purple velvet box, about the size of a coffee pot or a small blender. She handed it to Astrid, who brought it over to Willow with something of a solemn expression on her features.

"This," she said, "is the Orb of Gorimaan. It was forged by the drabardi in the fifth century, commissioned by the King of the Franks and found centuries later when pirates dug up his grave. It is said to have powers of divination beyond imagining and if used for malice, the one who wields it will go mad. Wars have been waged, blood spilled, and good men have turned to darkness to gain control over it. Until recently, when it came into our possession. Now I will pass it on to you."

Astrid raised the box above Willow's head with outstretched arms—Lion King style. And Willow had never jumped away from someone so fast in her life. Her heart leapt to her throat, her face pale as a sheet, and in tumbling over to the other side of the room, knocked over her chair and kicked the corner of an end table, causing it to wobble.

But Astrid only laughed—a small little laugh, really—and dipped her hand into the box to take out the crystal ball within.

Willow gasped and wished she was better at magic so she could poof out of there.

"Ah, Willow!" Astrid said with amusement. "I'm only joking. I picked this up at Hobby Lobby for twenty bucks on sale. But if you use that story, you'll bring in so much cash, your head will spin. Not literally spin. Figuratively spin. And did I tell you all proceeds go to charity? Children. Who can't read."

Willow was beside herself. And what kind of joke was that? She nearly peed her pants.

"I'm sorry. I didn't mean to frighten you," Astrid said in a gentler tone.

"So it's just a prop?" Willow asked.

Nadine hopped up and snapped the thing out of Astrid's hands. "Honestly, Astrid. Enough dramatics."

She turned the crystal ball over in her hands, touched the bottom of the base, and flipped it over for Willow to see.

There, stuck on the bottom of the trinket, was a sticker

price tag showing the sale price as nineteen ninety-nine. Then Nadine slipped it back into the velvet box and closed the lid.

"Even though it's not worth much," she said to Willow, "it's important you take very good care of it. Sure, we could buy a new one, but we need every penny for the children's charity. Will you do that, Willow?"

"Um, I suppose so. But I wouldn't know the first thing about fortune telling. I know a lot more about books…"

"Oh, it's super easy," Jewels said with a wave of her hand. "You just throw a scarf on your head, wear big hoop earrings, and make stuff up. People only want to hear that they'll be coming into some money in the future or will have everything they desire come true. Piece of cake. No offense, Rowena."

"None taken," Rowena said.

"Will you do it?" Nadine asked Willow. "It's a big money maker."

Willow bit her lip, and thought about what her mother would do. Esme not only would say yes, but she'd run the fortune telling booth with style.

"I'll do it," Willow said. "For the children."

"For the children," Jewels echoed.

"One last order of business," Nadine said, placing the velvet box at Willow's feet. "Willow's onboarding."

"My… onboarding?"

"Into the Mysthaven Women's Business Council, of course. It's just a pledge to honor our small-town values and our promise to hold each other up as women entrepreneurs. Rowena, do you have that paper?"

"I certainly do." Rowena plucked a half sheet of paper from the side table that Willow almost knocked over and handed it to Willow. "These are the guidelines. As you'll see, they're pretty straightforward."

"I'll say," Willow mused as she read the list of '*rules*' if you could call them that. "Be kind. If you can't say anything nice, don't say anything at all. You're never fully dressed without a smile. That's it?"

"That's it," Daria said. "Do you agree to these terms in order to be a member?"

Willow almost laughed. "I do."

"Perfect. I'll take the list back, now. It's my only copy." Daria pinched the corner and tugged it from Willow's hand, but as she did so, the edge of the paper sliced into Willow's thumb, leaving her with a thin gash.

"Ow," Willow cried and quickly sucked at the wound.

"I am so sorry," exclaimed Daria, taking hold of Willow's hand and pressing her own thumb over the papercut. "It's important to apply pressure. Trust me, I'm a medical professional."

Willow certainly couldn't argue with that, so she waited the few moments of thumb squeezing until Daria was finished.

"There. Good as new," Daria said.

Willow turned over her hand to look at her thumb, but the blood was gone, and there was barely a trace of a cut. In fact, she didn't see the cut at all.

"Huh," she wondered, squinting her eyes.

"The human body is a remarkable thing," said Daria.

Before Willow could examine her cut more closely, Jewels exclaimed, "Oh I almost forgot!"

She dug inside her pocket (because of course her dress would have pockets), and took out an oval thing made out of some kind of metal, probably stainless steel or silver. It had engravings of what looked like leaves or vines, and a decorative swirly pattern.

"Here you go," Jewels said, snapping it on Willow's wrist. "As part of the Women's Business Council, this bracelet entitles you to discounts all over Mysthaven. And always wear it, because when shop owners see it on you, they sometimes give you free stuff out of the blue."

"Really? Wow. Thank you."

"Oh I meant to tell you ladies," Rowena said, "I was in the market the other day and as I was checking out, Tom put a big bag of apples in my cart because he said he received more than he ordered. Such a nice man. Naturally, I made my famous apple tarts and brought one over to him the next day. He ate it on the spot. Right there on aisle four between the Rice-A-Roni and chicken noodle soup."

"Tom owns the market around the corner from your book store," Astrid said to Willow. "You'll get to know him."

"I can't even walk into Mysthaven Mercantile without them giving me something," Daria said. "Last week it was bolts of fabric. They said they had to make room for more inventory. Things like this happen all the time."

"That's amazing," Willow said. "Everyone is so nice here."

"The Women's Business Council does a lot for this town," Nadine said. "Discounts and the occasional gifts are their way of showing us their appreciation."

"I never take off my bracelet," Astrid said. "Not even in the shower."

"Neither do I," said Jewels.

Willow traced her fingers over the bracelet on her own wrist. "Then I won't either."

All the ladies seemed pleased and agreed the meeting was over because they had to start their workday. But then they stayed for another hour drinking more tea, nibbling on pastries, and chatting about their families or some town gossip.

Willow learned that Nadine had a son just out of high school who was going through a rebellious stage. The ladies tried to offer some comfort and advice to no avail. Then there was the woman who ran the local yoga studio who was too much of a flirt. There was also the town drunk who decided to drive his tractor down the main street when he lost his license. And apparently, the man who owned the diner was so disagreeable, he'd kick people out in the middle of their meals, so Willow should find somewhere else to eat. The food was reportedly mediocre anyway.

Willow's thoughts were still stuck on the tractor guy

though, and she wondered if he had green eyes and a penchant for handlebar mustaches.

With a full belly, full brain, and that velvet box in her bike basket, Willow went home to the bookshop in time to reflect on the morning's happenings before opening for the day.

Going in through the back door, she heard a noise coming from the front of the store as if something fell, hitting the floor with a clank. She hurried to investigate, but found nothing but a mop toppled over on the hardwood, the smell of lemony pine filling her nostrils. She picked it up, propping it against the wall wondering how it got there. Sure, she'd been deliriously tired last night and was super forgetful of late, but she would have remembered something like mopping the floor. And yet, it was sparkling clean, gleaming in the morning sunlight which filtered through the front windows.

A mewl took her attention from the mop, and she lifted her eyes to see Zephyr perched on top of a bookcase. She wandered over to him, setting the velvet box on the shelf between Poe and Proust.

"Hey, little guy." She reached up to gather the cat in her arms, scratching him between the ears. "*You* didn't mop the floor, did you?"

It wasn't entirely improbable. She'd heard of cat familiars that could shape shift into human form—usually for nefarious purposes. But Zephyr was just a regular cat.

Then it occurred to her. Astrid said her colleague's son needed a job and she would send him over. She didn't just give the guy a key, did she? People in this town were pretty friendly, but that was taking it a little too far, in Willow's opinion.

She reached for her cell phone to call Astrid, but the screen was doing something weird.

"Darn cell service," Willow muttered under her breath. Then, after trying to find reception all over the room, she unlocked the front door and went outside, where her phone worked immediately.

"Hmmm." Willow looked up the exterior of the building. "Must be all the brick."

She tapped on Astrid's contact who picked up immediately, and after the usual greetings, Willow asked her if she'd sent her colleague's son to work.

"I'm so sorry," Astrid said. "I meant to tell you this morning, but Nadine was so upset about her son, I didn't want to say anything else about it."

"Nadine's son?"

"Yes, he's the boy I was going to send to work for you, but he's been such trouble lately, he flat out refused. I'm sure it's no reflection on you. He's just being difficult, you know, and doesn't want anything to do with his mother or anyone associated with her. Kids these days. But I'll keep an eye out and if I hear of anyone looking for a job, I'll let you know."

"Thank you, Astrid. You've helped so much already. But are you sure he didn't come by? Maybe he had a change of mind?"

"I'm sure, dear. He's not even in Mysthaven at the moment."

Willow thanked her again and ended the call more perplexed than before. If Nadine's son didn't come over, and Zephyr was certainly just a cat, who on earth mopped the floor?

"DURING THE DAY,
I DON'T BELIEVE IN GHOSTS.
AT NIGHT, I'M A LITTLE MORE OPEN-MINDED."

-Unknown

Chapter Five

AN UNRULY MESS

Rain pelted against the windows, cleansing Willow's anxieties after another wildly exhausting day. The bookshop was bustling with so many customers, it was a wonder they didn't get upset with how long it took for her to serve them. But each and every person was patient, enjoying the cookies she'd baked while perusing the shelves for a new book to take home.

Now, as she lay under her covers, trying to decompress from the long day, she was grateful her business was booming, but had to hire someone as soon as possible. She rolled her eyes at herself for listening to Astrid in the first place, knowing she should have placed that announcement in the want ads days ago.

Bone weary, she nuzzled her head against her pillow, determined to get some sleep. But thoughts kept turning over in her head, how she might improve the customer experience from the moment they walked in the door to when they left—hopefully with bags of books in tow.

"I sure could use some ideas, Zephyr."

Turning to her side, she reached her arm over on the mattress expecting to find a ball of fur curled next to her, but the cat was sound asleep by her feet.

"You're no help at all," she whisper-hissed.

Then, closing her eyes, she let the patter of the rain drops calm her and thanked the muses it hadn't poured hard during the day, lest it ward off customers from venturing out.

She was just beginning to doze off, when the conscious part of her awareness noticed the din of water, but it wasn't coming from the storm outside. Halfway to dreaming, she thought it was the shower running, but no, that couldn't have been it. Her eyes shot open, and laying on her mattress perfectly still, she listened, narrowing down the echoing gurgle to what had to be the plumbing rattling within the house. With such thin walls, one could easily hear the humming of the water vibrating through the pipes when a faucet was turned on. But it was after midnight. And she was alone. It had to be nothing. Unless... Could it have been a leak? Did she accidentally keep the bar sink running?

Heart in her throat, she tuned her ears like a wolf towards the sound—loud banging followed by the gurgling whistle of running water. But it was the squealing of the pipes that made the hair on her arms stand on end.

Coupled with a sudden gust of wind howling beyond her window, and the boom of distant thunder, the knocks and taps of the creaky plumbing sent shivers down her spine.

Unnerved, she slowly crept out of bed, her palms sweating, her heart palpitating with a sinking sense of dread and foreboding.

As a precaution, she picked up the object closest to her —which happened to be her broom. A whole lot of help *that* would be in this situation. But she clung to it like a lifeline and opened her apartment door, willing it not to creak, and slowly tiptoed down the stairs, one shaky step at a time.

As she descended closer to the darkened hallway behind the shop, the sound of running water grew louder. But that wasn't the only sound. Taking the smallest steps with her stocking feet, she noticed a soft light spilling from the kitchen onto the hallway floor, and along with the steady stream of flowing water, the occasional splash, then the clang of a dish or ping of a wine glass.

Her heart lodged itself high in her throat, and she could hardly breathe as she stood stone still, back pressed ramrod straight against the wall leading into the kitchen.

It was here she wished she wasn't such a magical screw up. If she'd only tried harder, or taken basic incantations seriously. Whatever the source of the splashing and clanging coming from the kitchen, a little bit of magic would have come in handy. If it was an intruder, it might have been easy. If it was something more sinister, well... she'd be toast no matter what she tried.

Clinging to the broom handle, she directed her thoughts to the spark of magic within her—calling upon that part of her DNA which gave her gifts in the first place. She'd always thought witchcraft was frivolous, like it was somehow cheating in life. She didn't think it was fair to non-magical beings when warlock kind got ahead using spells and enchantments instead of good old hard work. She was often vocal about her ideals over dinner back home, and more recently, congratulated herself for her accomplishments without the aid of magic.

But right now, standing outside the kitchen in her pajamas, armed with nothing but a useless broom, she really was rethinking that high horse. If only she knew how to recreate that eyebrow singeing incident.

With more courage than she actually felt, she wiggled her fingers, trying spin a tiny bit of sorcery, took a deep breath, and leapt into the opening to the kitchen hollering, "Wazzah!"

She wasn't sure why she thought *wazzah* was appropriate in this circumstance, but once it was out, she went with it, and brandished her broom like a weapon.

But what she saw dispelled all feelings of fright, and replaced it with brimming vexation, and whatever sparkle of magic her fingers aroused, it was gone now.

"You!" she snarled.

There, standing in front of the sink, washing her dishes, was a man with a neat handlebar mustache, a crisp waistcoat, and eyes the brilliance and color of bioluminescent foxfire.

"Indeed," he replied with a lazy smile, his gaze catching on the broom. "Are you planning on using that thing or is it just for show?"

He didn't wait for an answer, returning to the dishes as though this was all perfectly normal.

Willow, so incredulous at the audacity of this man, stuttered as she pointed to the door. "G-g-get out!"

Montgomery paused in the middle of sudsy-sponging a highball glass, tilted his head without even looking at Willow, and simply said, "No."

"I'm serious," Willow cried. "Get out or I'll call the cops."

A humorless half-laugh escaped Montgomery's lips. "I don't think that's a wise idea."

"Why not?"

Then, setting the glass down in the sink, he gave her a hard stare over his shoulder. "Because they'll think you're out of your mind, and I'll still be here, watching you try to convince them that someone they can't see washed your dirty dishes and mopped the floor."

"It was you? *You* mopped my floor?"

"*My* floor, but let's not get caught up in the minutiae."

"Why?"

"Why what?"

"Why did you mop the floor? And why are you washing the dishes? Are you some kind of... cleaning bandit?"

He laughed, this time genuinely amused. If he wasn't so infuriating (and hadn't broken into her shop), the deep timbre of his laughter, and the hint of a dimple hiding behind that mustache, would have made Willow swoon a little.

"No, not a cleaning bandit," he said.

"Then why are you cleaning my dishes?"

"Because you are a slob. And frankly, it's driving me nuts."

"I beg your pardon?"

Willow sensed Montgomery didn't seem to care much for the trajectory of this conversation and was given further confirmation of this when he merely shook his head and resumed his work without saying another word.

"Wait. Back up a little. What did you mean when you said I'd *'be trying to convince the police that someone they can't see washed my dishes?'* Do you have some creepy hiding place I don't know about? Because I will smoke you out, sir."

He chuckled at that, rinsing off the glass, placing it on

the drying rack, and shutting off the faucet. Then, he turned to face her with smug confidence. "I'm afraid that would be an exercise in futility, Miss Ravensong. No matter how hard you try, your efforts to get rid of me will prove to be a disappointment at best."

"Oh? We'll see about that."

"I suppose we will."

"I have resources. If you lay one finger on me, mister—"

For some reason, that made Montgomery laugh the hardest.

"I can tell you with one hundred percent certainty that I will *never* lay a finger on you," he said.

Willow wasn't sure whether to be offended or relieved by that statement. After some thought, she decided not to believe it.

"You never answered my question about your creepy hiding place where you sneakily watch people." She gasped. "Have you been in my bedroom?"

"No, I don't have a hiding place and I don't watch anyone with unsavory motives—much less your private quarters. Believe me, I just wish I could have some peace and quiet."

"Then I recommend you go home. Right now. If you leave now, I won't press charges. And I have security cameras with facial recognition technology, so they'd find out who you really are... *Montgomery*. If that's even your real name."

Willow wasn't sure if the cameras had facial recognition or not. She just made that up, actually. But in her mind, this intruder didn't have to know it.

Montgomery crossed his arms over his chest causing the fabric of his linen shirt to stretch over the sculpted girth of his upper arm.

"Like I told you before, that's not going to happen."

Willow forced her gaze away from his broad chest and stuck out her chin. "I feel like we're just going around in circles here."

A pregnant pause descended upon the room as Montgomery narrowed his eyes, studying Willow with equal parts curiosity and wonder. That look. It almost made her tummy flip. Almost.

At length, he asked, "What makes you so special?"

"Excuuuuse me?"

Suddenly, the temporary insanity of Willow's fancies evaporated into a puff of righteous indignation, and she gave her male intruder a scowl that could peel paint off the walls.

But that didn't stop his scrutinizing stare. "Who *are* you?"

"I'm the one who's gonna whoop your hipster butt, that's who."

He pressed his eyes shut, pinching a thumb and forefinger between his brows. "I'm not even going to dignify that with a response."

"Because you're afraid of me."

"I am definitely not afraid of you."

Willow raised the broom to the level of her face. "You should be."

"How is it that you seem to be the only living person... who can see me?"

"Okay, I know what this is. You're a nut job. Or my sisters put you up to this." She shouted to the heavens as if her sisters could hear her. "Not cool, Ivy and Bliss!"

"You can see me... and you can talk to me. Fascinating." He took a step toward her. "Can you touch me?"

Willow thrust the broom more pointedly at him. "Stay right there!"

"I need to know," he said, drawing closer by degrees.

"I swear I will hurt your face," she cried.

His feet halted, but the expression on his face and the rest of his body language were fully engaged, like he'd pounce any second.

"Do it," he said, daring her to act.

"What?"

"Do. It. Hit me with your '*deadly*' weapon. Hit me as hard as you can."

"I'm not an idiot. Do you think I'm just going to swing because you told me to? That completely eliminates the element of surprise."

He let out a hard sigh. "You are singularly the most insufferable woman I have ever met."

"I'll take that as a compliment."

"Listen, I give you my word, I have no intention of molesting you."

Willow threw him a sassy glare. "Sure. You just stopped by to do my dishes."

"Miss Ravensong..."

"How do I know you don't have a gun?"

"I'm going to turn around now, and you're going to hit me."

"I mean who does that? What kind of weirdo breaks into a closed bookshop-slash-bar to... clean it?"

"Hit me, woman. I won't ask again."

"Seriously. The sheer cheek!"

A stormy growl permeated from the depths of Montgomery's throat. His features paled, and if possible, his eyes seemed to glow even greener.

"I wouldn't have to clean if you didn't make such an unruly mess," he said through gritted teeth.

"Listen here, buddy. This *unruly mess* is my business, not yours. I happen to like my mess. I plan on making more messes. If you don't like it, don't come here."

"Unbelievable. Over a hundred and ten years, not a soul to talk to, and *you're* the one I'm stuck with."

"You're a neat freak, aren't you? Some kind of vigilante? Righting the wrongs of the world's dirt?" With the broom still in one hand, Willow shuffled sideways to the refrigerator, took out a container of Bloody Mary mix, and tilted it just enough so the liquid barely touched the mouth of the bottle. "I'll do it."

He stretched out his hand. "No!"

"Nah, ah, ah!" Willow stepped just out of his reach.

"Take your funky mustache out of this place or the floor gets it."

"You wouldn't."

"I would. And I'll bet it drives you soooo crazy."

"That would be a waste of perfectly sellable tomato juice." His voice lowered to a sinister tone. "Your profit margin would go down."

Willow raised one eyebrow—in the same way Ivy did but without the ability to use it for magic—and tilted the bottle in her hand, spilling a small amount of mix onto the floor.

Montgomery gasped, which encouraged Willow to do it again—this time, a longer pour and with a sinister grin spread across her features. Montgomery's mouth dropped and his eyes practically bulged out of his head.

"You're mad," he said incredulously. "Certifiably mad."

Willow's smile grew wider, wickedly devilish, and she tipped the container dramatically, sploshing peppery red juice all over the floor, making an enormous puddle. Montgomery lunged, probably trying to get to a mop, but his sudden movement alarmed Willow, and out of reflex, she threw the bottle at him. But it didn't bounce off his chest as it should have. It went right through him as if he weren't even there.

"What the...?"

Montgomery didn't appear to be surprised. In fact, he tossed up his arms in disappointment and sighed when he said, "Oh well."

But Willow wasn't so calm. At first, she stared at him

in cold shock, and then once she registered what happened, let out a delayed scream.

The screaming was accompanied with finger flexing as she tried to conjure some magic. Any magic. And when nothing sparked from her efforts, she resorted to wild swings of her broom. But every single swoosh and swish that should have smacked the daylights out of Montgomery the cleaning bandit, didn't make contact with him at all.

"You might as well stop trying," said Montgomery with a note of resignation.

Willow, still in a manic state, gripped the broom handle to her chest. On the verge of hyperventilating, she stuttered, "You're a... you're a..."

He nodded with a slight eye roll, as though annoyed with his current state of being, and replied, "A ghost."

And in the next moment, he disappeared from her sight.

"BEING A WITCH MEANS
LIVING IN THIS WORLD
CONSCIOUSLY, POWERFULLY,
AND UNAPOLOGETICALLY."

-Gabriela Herstik

Chapter Six

PUT THAT THING BACK
WHERE IT CAME FROM
OR SO HELP ME!

Anything can appear differently in the cold light of day. Nightclubs, for instance. They're pretty cool plunged in darkness, where a potential romantic paramour will seem a true good looker with nothing but neon lights to recommend them.

But the following morning? Yikes.

After a mild freak out and hiding under her covers

until her eyes burned with fatigue, Willow got exactly one hour and twenty-three minutes rest, waking up groggy in the way that one does when they don't remember where they are or what day of the week it is. How they hang on to sleep when the veil between dreaming and waking is as thin as spider silk. How they cling to the memory of that dream, willing it to last longer for the beautiful, strange feeling of it.

Willow liked the strange feeling of dreams—that lucid state of awareness where she could be someone else. It was much like getting lost in a book.

But whatever she dreamed the night before was something she'd rather forget. And as the window's daylight washed across her face and awareness dawned on her, she began to question if she'd dreamt it at all. Did she really encounter a ghost last night?

Zephyr tapped relentlessly at her arm demanding breakfast, and Willow realized in a panic she'd missed her alarm, leaving seven minutes before opening the bookshop. Rushing to brush her teeth, toss on some jeans, and feed the cat left her no time to even think about whether her shop was actually haunted or not. In fact, dashing downstairs to prep the store with only a couple minutes to spare, she'd almost forgotten about it. That is until a resonant male voice startled her to such an extreme, her heart almost stopped.

"Miss Ravensong?"

With a terrified shriek she almost jumped high enough to hit the ceiling. When she turned toward the voice, there stood Montgomery Harland, looking very much the same as before—with that same old-fashioned vest and that ridiculous mustache. What really irked her was that he didn't even look like a ghost at all. He looked... well, very much like a man who'd been present all night while she slept... and that thought aroused her more than it unnerved her. She cursed inwardly, blaming her stupid non-existent dating life for letting her imagination go there.

Clutching her chest, Willow snapped, "Are you trying to kill me?"

"And run the risk of being stuck with you for all eternity? I think not."

"Hmmm. Even your snark wasn't a figment of my imagination."

"Nor was the sticky tomato atrocity on the kitchen floor."

Right. Willow had forgotten about that—what, with the ghost thing and all.

"Why are you still here?" she questioned, not wanting to think about the Bloody Mary mess on the kitchen floor. "Didn't you dip out last night? You scared the bejeezus out of me, made the announcement 'I'm a ghost', and then poof. Gone."

"I have no control over how or when I enter consciousness," he said. "Maybe it's triggered by vexatious red-haired women."

Willow snorted. "Vexatious. You need to spend less time in the thesaurus section."

Montgomery raised his gaze to the ceiling, shaking his head. "Nevertheless, I'll have you know that I've taken care of the spill in the kitchen, and I would appreciate it if you would refrain from causing more mayhem." He inclined his head toward the front entrance where there was a man waiting outside. "Now... I believe you have a customer. I'll just be sitting over there."

In a panic, Willow said, "I won't let you stick around and haunt my customers. You need to go."

"Nobody can see or hear me but you. And also, your cat." He flicked his hand at the door. "You better open up shop before he takes his business elsewhere."

With that, he slipped a book off the shelf and made himself comfortable in the same wingback chair he sat in on opening day.

Infuriated, but out of arguments, Willow hurried over to unlock the door and flip over the sign to display the *'Come in we're an open book'* side.

She plastered on a cheery smile and greeted the customer, all the while keeping a side eye on the ghost in the corner. The skin on her palms was relentlessly clammy the whole while she was helping the customer find what he was looking for, and at one point, she had to think hard to remember if she'd used deodorant this morning.

After the man left with his purchase, Willow doubled over by the cash register, breathing heavily.

"There's a ghost in my shop. There's a ghost in my shop. I'm freaking out. There's a ghost in my shop."

"You need not cause yourself anxiety," Montgomery

said casually flipping the page of his book. "I told you they can't see me. And I don't plan on spooking them if that's what you're worried about."

Willow's head shot up with an idea. "I'll call my mom. She'll know what to do."

She dialed the phone with shaking fingers, but Esme didn't pick up, so she texted in all caps.

Willow: CALL ME

She glanced over at Montgomery, wondering at how a dead guy could be so apathetic to his plight. Shouldn't ghosts be moaning and wailing or something?

Zephyr weaved around Montgomery's feet—every so often his tail or his hind leg passing through a leg where it should have rubbed against it. The cat settled finally, looking up at the man and meowed for attention until Montgomery momentarily abandoned his book to acknowledge the cat.

"I wish I could pet you, my good fellow. But alas, I am not a corporeal being."

Willow grimaced at Montgomery. "How can you wash dishes and sit in that chair but you can't pet a cat? It makes no sense."

"You are asking questions I have no more ability to answer than fly to the moon. I can only guess, as everything in the universe is made of energy, the energy of inanimate objects manifests differently than in living creatures. I am still made up of energy. And after some practice, I was able to direct it to control certain types of matter."

"Like a poltergeist," Willow said.

"I can only presume so."

"Great. So instead of throwing things or leaving drawers and cabinets open, I get the only poltergeist in history who's a neat freak."

Montgomery sniffed dismissively and returned to his book. "I like my surroundings clean and tidy."

A sharp comeback was on the tip of Willow's tongue but her phone rang, so she decided to pocket her witty words for later.

"Mother! Why didn't you pick up before?"

"It took me a minute to find where I hid the phone." Esme laughed. "It was in my cedar chest of all places."

"Why did you hide the cell phone I bought you?"

"You know I don't like these things. You could have just as easily used an easy mirror charm to contact me."

Willow cringed at the memory of the broken mirror the last time she tried to use a mirror charm to summon someone. Seven years bad luck for the cracks. Only the Fates know what the consequence was for causing that mysterious black smoke.

"Just keep the phone close to you. This is important. I need your help."

Bliss's voice echoed from somewhere in the room

Esme was in. "It's the herb garden, isn't it? I knew she'd kill those plants."

"It's not the herb garden," Willow said, rolling her eyes. "It's something else."

Willow heard Esme mumble something to Bliss, then a door creaked shut.

"You can speak freely, now," Esme said in a whisper. And even though Willow appreciated the effort, she knew her sisters had ways of eavesdropping on any phone conversation. But at this point, she didn't really mind.

"Okay, not to alarm you or anything but... I'm being haunted."

Esme was silent for a moment before saying, "You're going to have to be more specific, Pumpkin."

"I don't know how to be more specific than that. There is a ghost in my shop, and I'm being haunted."

"Oh. Well then. That *is* something. Hmmm."

"What should I do?"

"That depends," Esme said. "You could do nothing, or you could help it move on."

"Help it move on. Definitely that."

"Good choice. The first thing you need to do is draw it out. A seance for instance."

"Ewww. No. I don't do stuff like that."

"Alright, alright. It was only a suggestion. But if you have a haunt, as frightening as it may sound, you need to draw it into the light. Make it communicate—show itself."

"Oh, he's shown himself, alright."

"He?"

Willow gritted her teeth. "He's sitting right over there. With a smug look on his face."

"Interesting. And how are your customers reacting?"

"No one else can see or hear him. At least that's what he says."

"Ooooh. You're like... Whoopie Goldberg in *Ghost*. Please tell me he looks like Patrick Swayze."

"More like... Jude Law in the *Sherlock Holmes* movie kind of vibe."

"Sherlock Holmes?" Montgomery popped his head up from his book. "I've read the work of Arthur Conan Doyle. Quite entertaining."

"Nobody asked you, Slimer. Go back to your book."

"Slimer?" questioned Esme.

"Never mind that. How do I get rid of him?"

"Ghosts are rarely here by choice and are sometimes confused... or don't even know they're not alive anymore. You need to find out why he is in this realm. Perhaps he has some unfinished business."

Willow knew this ghost was quite aware he was dead, and seemed to stick around just for the fun of vexing her, but she asked anyway.

"My mom wants to know if you have any unfinished business."

Montgomery glowered back at her. "Unfinished business? Why yes."

"Really? What is it?" Willow, anxious to get the whole thing over with, was eager to hope they'd be done by tea time. "Tell me."

"He said yes?" Esme asked, only able to hear Willow's side of the conversation. "You're making fast progress, Willow. I'm so proud of you."

"What unfinished business do you have?" Willow pressed.

Montgomery's eyes glittered. "This book. Now if you'll keep it down over there, I can find out what happens to Frodo and his friends."

"How 'bout I spoil the ending and we'll call it a day?" Willow snapped.

"What did he say?"

"He's reading *Lord of the Rings*."

"Curiouser and curiouser. Which book is he on?"

"Hey. Watson. What's happening to Frodo right now?"

He rolled his eyes and grunted. "If you must know, the hobbits are dining at Tom Bombadil's house."

"Yeesh. This could take a while. He's only a few chapters in on book one."

Montgomery gasped. "Book *one*? You mean to tell me there are more?"

"Esme, please tell me I can spoil it for him."

Montgomery shot up from the chair. "How many books exactly?"

"One more peep out of you, mister, and I'll subject you to the Peter Jackson movies."

"He sure seems to be a chatty one," said Esme. "I'll search in my library for banishing spells. Your sisters packed a grimoire in your luggage. You might find some incantations between the pages to send your unwanted spirit back across the veil, or at least repress the hauntings. I'll summon you in a couple days to check on you. In the meantime, research everything you can on this person. Who they were, how they died, if there was a shady business deal or a so-called friend who wanted Demi Moore all to himself."

"I gotta go, Mom. He's rummaging through the shelves looking for more Tolkien. There are six books, Montgomery. Seven if you count *The Children of Hurin*. Put that special edition down right now or so help me..."

"Are you going to be okay, Willow? This ghost of yours seems dangerous. All that reading and Jude Law smolder."

"There is no smolder. Just a false sense of superiority and probably an excess of ectoplasm."

"Okay, love. I'll keep this horrible cell phone near me in case you call. But if it gets out of hand, promise you'll come home."

"It won't come to that. But if it does, I promise I'll come home. Love you."

Willow pressed the screen to end the call (because her mother always left it on) and opened her laptop to search the web for any and all information on Montgomery Harland. And if the ghost in front of her would cooperate, she might make some headway to exorcizing him from her bookshop.

So, she decided she'd start from the end, asking Montgomery point blank, and feeling a little bit spooked out saying, "What year did you die?"

"HALLOWEEN IS THE ONLY TIME
PEOPLE CAN BECOME WHAT THEY WANT TO BE
WITHOUT GETTING FIRED."

— Sylvester Stallone

Chapter Seven

STRANGE THINGS ARE AFOOT AT THE CIRCLE-K

It was a three-pill kind of day. Normally, Willow shunned ibuprofen and would power through a headache by guzzling an extra glass of water and doing some deep, restorative breathing. But after two restless nights, this headache was a doozy. Not quite a migraine, but migraine adjacent.

And everybody knows the best cure for a migraine

adjacent headache (besides Advil) is a serious vat of coffee and chocolate chip pancakes. It's the chocolate that makes them so healthy. Besides, Willow needed to get out of the shop before the clean freak drove her bonkers. If something was even a little bit out of place, he'd fix it. If he wasn't already dead, she'd have killed him herself.

So, not wanting to take up one of the tables at Bo's Diner, she sat at the bar and was treated to a front row seat to the chaotic workings of a busy food establishment. It was fascinating to see, how with only a cook to assist him, this Bo guy could keep up with so many food orders and maintain his sanity.

He was handsome, Willow noticed as she stuffed herself with fluffy, syrupy carbs. With piercing blue eyes, broad shoulders, and a chiseled jaw that hadn't seen a razor in a few days, Bo looked like he'd be right at home in the wilderness, hunting for his dinner. His wavy, dark brown hair peeked out from underneath a trucker hat with a drawing of a fish on the front, and his thick forearms broadcasted to anyone within a hundred yards that he was of sturdy build and probably didn't do things like cross his legs while reading.

"Another refill?" Bo asked Willow, sliding behind the counter while multitasking a hundred other things.

"Since you asked so nicely," she replied. And as he poured, she took in the ruggedness of his features, how tanned his skin, with friendly lines around his eyes—such a contrast to the smooth, pearlescent face haunting her home.

She scolded herself for giving that ghost another thought, and reached for the sugar.

"You like it really sweet," Bo observed but quickly added, "Which is fine. I like sugar, too."

"As you should," said Willow. "Sugar is the one true sign of civilization."

"I'm Bo, by the way."

"I know."

Bo set down the coffee canteen and leaned on the counter as if Willow was the only customer in the diner. "You're the new owner of the old saloon on the corner. Willow, right?"

"Yes. News travels fast in a small town."

"Not used to small towns, then?"

"Actually, I'm from Crescent Hollow, about two hours northeast, and you could fit the whole town inside Mysthaven with room to spare."

"I've been to Crescent Hollow," Bo said, brightening. "I love that Salem vibe they've got going on over there. Ever run across any witches?"

"Witches?" Alarm bells rang in Willow's head. "What on earth would give you that idea?"

Crescent Hollow had one of the most populous witch communities in North America, but they kept to themselves and preferred their presence to be thought of as merely myths. Nobody in her hometown cared for unwanted attention.

"Just a little joke, that's all," Bo said with a laugh. "They seem to embrace the Halloween spirit even more than we do in Mysthaven. And this town goes all out, believe me."

"Yes, I've heard the Harvest Festival is a big deal. You were in charge of planning in the past?"

Bo's features darkened. "No. That was my father, Bo senior. I don't participate."

His eyes seemed to glass over as he stared into the middle distance, hurt etched across his features. Willow knew better than to press him, so she polished off the last bite of her pancakes and rubbed her belly in an almost cartoonish way.

"Mmm, you sure know how to make a mean flapjack, though."

This was encouragement enough for Bo to crack a charming smile, and he leaned onto the bar even more, his elbows resting mere inches from Willow's plate.

"I'm glad you like them. I hope I can make my pumpkin pancakes with cinnamon butter for you tomorrow."

Then, he winked, and the corner of his mouth curved up exposing truly nice teeth.

Was he flirting with her?

If so, she should have felt that warm rush sweeping up from her toes. Bo was the manifestation of any girl's dream with that virile way about him in all his lumber-jackness. She should flirt back. She really should. But she just wasn't feeling up to the task. Even after those wonderful pancakes.

"Have you lived here long?" she asked instead, feeling

that she should get all the information she could about this town's history.

"All my life," he replied.

"Oh that's great. Did the previous owner of the bar ever come in here?"

She wanted to add *"And did they ever mention it was haunted?"* but thought better of it.

"Probably. I don't know. I was just a kid when it closed down. It's been vacant ever since. Over twenty years now."

"Wow. That's a long time. I'll bet there's a lot of history there, as old as it is. If only the walls could talk, ha." She forced a little laugh. "I'm sure *you* could tell me some stories."

Montgomery had told her he was the original owner, but it turns out, ghosts have memories like swiss cheese. He couldn't tell her much more than she'd found on the internet. That it opened in 1908, and closed after the untimely, but natural death of the owner on October 31, 1912—one Mr. Montgomery Harland.

"If there are stories, I wouldn't know," said Bo. "Except that every time it came close to selling, something fell through with the buyers. Either they couldn't get financing or just lost interest. Until you came around. That's why everyone is so thrilled to see it open up again."

"Well, I'm sorry it was vacant for such a long time," Willow said sincerely. "But maybe it was meant to be. And I promise to make it a welcoming place for the towns-people to have a cocktail and read books."

That was, she thought, as long as no one knew the

place was haunted. She imagined *that* little fact would be bad for business. "I just wish I knew more of the history."

"You know," Bo said. "The property records are available to the public, if you really want to know everything about that old building."

"Really?"

"Sure. I actually have to go down to the county registrar in a few days to file some permits for this place. I could look through the archives for you while I'm there."

"That would be wonderful, Bo. I appreciate it."

Willow marveled at how friendly the people were in this town, noting the twinkle in Bo's eye.

"Excuse me," said a voice behind her, accompanied by a pointy tap on her shoulder. "Are you Willow Ravensong?"

Bo jabbed a finger at the person behind Willow. "Dale, I've told you a hundred times. Leave my customers alone."

"I'm here in a professional capacity, Bo," said the guy that Willow now knew was named Dale.

She turned to face him and was met with the slender, clean-shaven face of a young man who was probably older than he looked. He wore a button-down shirt covered by a threadbare sweater, and sensible beige slacks.

Bo grumbled. "If you're not here to eat, then get out."

"I'll have a Cherry Coke please," Dale said quickly, then sat down on the stool next to Willow.

Bo mumbled something under his breath and shuffled over to the soda machine.

Dale held out his hand to Willow. "I'm Dale Dune.

Perhaps you've heard of me. I hold the record for Mysthaven's bubble gum chewing contest. It's kind of a big deal."

Shaking Dale's hand, Willow smiled warmly. "I'm afraid I haven't had the pleasure."

"You should probably get out more," he replied. "There's a plaque on the gazebo."

Bo returned then, plunking the soda on the counter with a hard thud.

"*You* put that plaque there," he said sternly. "And the only reason it's still there is because nobody wants to have to pay to fix the wood where the screws are."

"I know you're just jealous, Bo. It takes a lot of air in your lungs to be able to blow that many bubbles."

"I think that's something I'd like to see," said Willow.

With a smug expression, Dale slipped a straw in his Cherry Coke, took a sip, then winced.

"Bo. This isn't Cherry Coke. This is regular Coke with cherry flavoring."

"It's the same thing," Bo said with a slight growl.

"No. It is definitely not the same thing," Dale countered. "*This* is a Roy Rogers. Big difference. Except you forgot the maraschino cherries on top."

"Would you like a maraschino cherry, Dale? Would *that* make you happy?"

Dale paused as if this was his most important decision of the day, then with a single nod, said, "Yes. Yes it would. But make it three cherries."

Bo sulked off into the back storeroom, probably in

search of a jar of cherries. Dale slid the glass away from him, waiting for his drink to be garnished, and leaned one elbow on the counter, facing Willow with a weighty look.

"So," he said resolutely. "What did you think of my email?"

"Your... email?"

"Yes. I sent you an email this morning regarding the job you posted on Craigslist. Took me all night to compose it."

Willow had only posted the listing before she went to bed. She hadn't expected such a speedy response.

"I... I'm sorry, but I haven't checked my email yet."

"Hmmm, I guess you were too busy. Understandable. I think you'll find my application more than adequate. I have extensive experience in retail work, as well as juggling, riding a unicycle, a thorough knowledge of skin-care, and I can play the bagpipes."

"The bagpipes? I've never met anyone who played the bagpipes before."

"Nor do you want to," Bo said, returning with an entire bowl of cherries. "They're loud and off key."

"They aren't off key," Dale argued. "The droning sound plays continuously throughout the melody."

He then addressed Willow conspiratorially. "Bagpipes are my secret to having lungs strong enough to be the bubble gum champion."

Willow decided that made a lot of sense and rather thought she'd like to hear Dale play the bagpipes. Chewing bubble gum, not so much.

"What are your favorite songs to play?" she asked.

"Most pipers' go-to is *Scotland the Brave* or *Danny Boy*. But I like to play tunes a little less traversed."

"Like what?"

Bo raised his eyes to the ceiling. "Here we go."

"You could say I have eclectic taste," Dale said. "*Blue Suede Shoes*, for instance. Also, *Suavamente Besa Me* is on my list of favorites."

"That *is* eclectic," Willow said, trying to imagine those songs performed on bagpipes. "I'm afraid I don't have a need in my store for a bagpiper, or juggler..."

Unless those skills could make a certain ghost go away.

"Don't forget my tremendous retail sales prowess. I can upsell like no other."

"Well..."

"I can vouch for him," Bo said in a surprising turn of events. "He might annoy the heck out of me, but he's a hard worker."

"Really?" Willow looked at Bo for confirmation of his sincerity. But Bo only sighed and bounced his head.

"Yes, actually. Dale is nothing if not reliable. Ridiculous as all get out. But reliable."

"Okay then." Willow wasn't one to argue with that, especially since she was in the weeds at the shop and in desperate need of help. "Can you start this afternoon?"

"I got the job?"

"You got the job," she said. "I have some business to take care of this morning, but I can start training after lunchtime."

She didn't admit her *'business'* involved driving out an irritating poltergeist, or at least convincing him to make himself scarce.

"I'll be there with bells on," Dale said proudly. "Well, not literal bells. Which is another one of my musical talents, but that will have to wait until Christmas."

"Can't wait," Willow said, and Dale took that as his cue to leave, which he did with a thumbs up.

"You didn't pay for your Roy Rogers," Bo shouted, but Dale was already out the door.

"You can put it on my bill," said Willow, but Bo waved his hand back, shaking his head.

"It's fine. I'm keeping tabs for when the guy finally wins the lottery."

"Oh yeah?"

"Yep. If anyone in Mysthaven ever wins, it'll be him. The guy's got the weirdest luck."

"Okay then," said Willow, then checking the time, realized she'd been in the diner too long and had stuff to do before opening the shop. "I'll take my check now, please."

And then remembering her Women's Business Council discount, showed Bo the bracelet.

"I... haven't tried using this yet, but I was told I could get discounts?"

Bo scowled at it like the bracelet itself had somehow offended him. "I don't honor that," he said. And Willow felt like an idiot. But then Bo softened toward her, and placed his warm palm over her hand as she reached for her wallet.

"First breakfast is on the house, though. For you."

Willow felt the weight of those words. *For you.* Not for the Women's Council, but only for her.

The gesture wasn't going to earn him a date or anything, but it was nice just the same. Perhaps she could extend him the same generosity if he went into her bookshop.

"Thank you," she said simply, not wanting to complicate things by insisting to pay. Esme always taught her to accept the kindness of others without a fuss. Instead of saying, "Are you sure?" or "Oh, you don't have to do that." Esme taught her to just say thank you and let them know it was appreciated.

As she left the diner, feeling pretty good about crossing a new hire off her to-do list, and making a friend in Bo, she had a spring in her step, striding down the sidewalk on her way back to Moonstone Spirits and Books. But she hadn't made it far before she almost ran into the tall figure of a man who'd stepped out in front of her from behind a display of pumpkins outside the grocery market.

"Oh, pardon me," she said, jerking to the side to get out of his way. But he only mirrored her movement, blocking her path.

She slid again to bypass him, but his presence was imposing, and she knew he was purposely trying to impede her by the way he scowled directly into her eyes.

"Willow Ravensong," said the stranger. It wasn't a

question of her identity. More of an ominous statement. An *'I know you'* omen or something.

"Have we met?" Willow asked, only a little frightened. After all, after meeting a real ghost, she didn't spook easily.

But the man didn't answer her, only narrowed his eyes inauspiciously, glaring at her with cold suspicion.

He had unruly, dark hair that whipped in the wind, tossing across his thin, pale face. He kind of reminded her of that actor from Dune—Timotay Shablagoo, or whatever that guy's name was...

"Something unholy is afoot," he warned in a low tone. "Stay away."

Willow blinked, thinking he could have the decency to at least be less cryptic, and opened her mouth to tell him so. But in the space of a heartbeat, he turned back behind the pumpkins—and was gone before she could follow.

"I THINK THAT
ALL WOMEN ARE WITCHES,
IN THE SENSE THAT
A WITCH IS A MAGICAL BEING."

-Yoko Ono

Chapter Eight

THE CAT CAME BACK

He felt the storm of her approach before she barged in from wherever she was... probably in the kitchen baking something sweet as she usually did before opening the shop. Montgomery had never seen such confections. Whether it be browned butter pumpkin oatmeal cookies or mini apple cider donuts, everything she made was a small masterpiece. And she gave it all away with a smile to anyone who walked into the shop.

That smile.

She was generous with her smiles to everyone but him. He would not be the recipient of tender looks, or even a disinterested glance. The best he could hope for were her scowls.

It was always something with that woman, and Montgomery braced himself for yet another shouting match. When Willow came into view, he was momentarily stunned by what he could only describe as a supernatural glow in her wake. Her feet leaving trails of stars, her hair the color of fire, and her skin, so radiant and flush, he could almost feel the warmth brimming off her.

"That's it," she cried. "One of us has to go and we both know who."

He replaced the book he was looking at back on the shelf and turned to face her with a smirk.

"It's about time you concede, Miss Ravensong. How soon can you pack your bags?"

"Not me Ghostface! You."

"I'm afraid that's not possible."

She waved her phone charger in her fist. "Why was this in the trash?"

"Exposed wire. You could burn the building down."

"Don't throw my stuff in the trash. And speaking of trash." She waved a foil take-out container in the other hand. "Don't dig things *out* of the trash, either. This is disposable. It's trash. My phone charger is not." She alternated raising one hand then the other. "Trash. Not trash. Trash. Not trash!"

"One thing is useful, the other is not," he replied.

"I am tired of you moving my things around. I like the way I have the furniture. It's called feng shui. Waking up to rearranged furniture creeps me out. Also, I have the well drink bottles in the speed rack for easy access. Keep them there. And another thing. The index cards on my desk. I spent twenty-five minutes putting them back in order."

Montgomery gave her a hard look. "They were spread out on the floor."

"Because I ran out of room on my desk! That is how my brain works. I need visual aids."

"I noticed my name written on many of the cards," he said then, "Coupled with a few expletives."

"Well, the internet wasn't helping much with my research and I got mad. Besides, how would you feel if you were being haunted?"

Montgomery wasn't keen on the idea of him being someone who'd haunt people. It took him years to come to terms with being dead. To him, he was just there, and as long as he wasn't doing spooky things, he didn't consider himself a nuisance.

"Truly, this is not what you'd call a conventional haunting," he said, hoping to get back to his books.

But Willow huffed, and threw up her arms. "Worse, actually. It's like living with a regular tedious man but without the benefits."

"And living with a messy woman is any easier?" he countered.

"Newsflash. You are not living. *You* have shuffled off your mortal coil. I'm alive. You're dead. I just bought this place. *You've* been hanging around for over a century." She slammed the contents in her hands onto a low shelf. "So go haunt the pharmacy down the street, or the hardware store, because I am so done."

Clearly, his books would have to wait, so he slid up to her, toe to toe.

"Oh, I would if I could, just to get away from you and your piles of papers. And the hair! Hair everywhere!"

"Then go, if you can't stand me that much. Go!"

"I can't leave the property. I've tried. I am stuck between these walls like an invisible prisoner."

She rolled her eyes and crossed her arms. "Are all ghosts this dramatic or just you?"

"I have never met another untethered spirit. Do you think we all gather on weekends to discuss the latest haunting methods?"

"No. Because you are a curmudgeon and don't play nicely with others."

Montgomery felt there was no other way to convince this woman that he was actually stuck in the building. He couldn't even go out into the alley.

"Open the door," he said. "Invite me to leave. Maybe, by some strange turn of luck, it will work this time."

Willow didn't need to be told twice. She was all too eager to send him away. If only it was that easy.

She flung the door open and swooshed her arm to the side. "Do I need to say special words?"

And she was the one calling *him* dramatic.

"Do you know Latin?" he said, more teasing than anything.

"A little Sanskrit, will that do?"

"Just tell me I'm not wanted or something like that."

"With pleasure." Willow closed her eyes intently, raising her palms above her head, and when she spoke, it was a performance worthy of the Globe Theatre. She began to chant in an over-the-top olde English cadence.

"Oh spirit, oh spirit. Thou art not welcome here."

"Is the English accent really necessary?"

"Shhh. I'm trying to concentrate." She cleared her throat and continued in the same fashion. "I cast thee from these lands. Leave us, and never return."

The woman was off her rocker. She had to be. And yet, he found her exceedingly fascinating.

After a pregnant pause, she opened one eye and repeated between her teeth, "Leave us, and never return."

"Oh, now?"

"Yes. Sheesh."

"I wasn't sure if you were done."

And so, with determination to make this work at last, he stepped through the threshold, and like every time he had attempted it in the past, was shot backwards with an invisible force, and landed ten feet away on his backside.

Willow, of course, laughed.

"You really *are* stuck here. Sam Wheat could travel all over the city but you can't."

"Sam Wheat?" Montgomery picked himself off the floor.

"It's from a movie called *Ghost*. Esme loves it. Correction—Esme loves Patrick Swayze. *Dirty dancing, Point Break, To Wong Foo, Thanks for Everything, Julie Newmar...*"

"Let me get this straight. You're basing all your assumptions about ghosts... from a movie?"

"In my defense, I thought you were just being stubborn."

It was his turn to laugh now.

"I hate to say I told you so but... Actually, I rather like saying I told you so."

He laughed maniacally in his best ghost imitation, which woke Zephyr, who'd been napping in the bookshelves. The cat yawned and stretched, then hopped down to purr at Montgomery's feet.

"Traitor," Willow snapped. "Just remember who feeds you."

"That would be me," said Montgomery.

"You feed my cat? He's going to get fat by eating double."

"Oh I pour that atrocious dry food back in the bag. He doesn't like it."

"Are you kidding me right now? What are you feeding him instead?"

"Usually chicken and whatever vegetables you have left over."

"Unbelievable. You're just a regular Bobby Flay, aren't you?"

Montgomery sniffed derisively. "You may wax poetic about Patrick Swayze or this Bobby fellow, or any other of your male suitors for all I care, but I am just a poor soul who never sleeps. And now you have a happy cat. You're welcome."

Willow snorted. "Male suitors. Your mind would go there, wouldn't it? Still in the dark ages where a woman is nothing without a husband."

She stalked toward him hotly, and even though he knew she'd just walk right through him if she continued, he backed away by degrees until she was close enough to slap him if she wanted to.

"Oh how we lie around all day on our fainting couches, darning socks and waiting for a gentleman caller," she continued, still advancing and he, still shuffling backward.

"Darning socks is a good skill to have," he said pragmatically, although Willow didn't seem to be in a mood to be reasoned with.

"And I suppose you think a woman should stay home scrubbing toilets and folding her husband's underwear," she said. "And when he gets home from work, she should have dinner ready, put a cocktail in his hand, and look like a pinup girl."

Montgomery sensed a tall bookshelf behind him and braced himself for contact. "What is a pinup girl?"

He could have shifted his energy to pass through the shelf, leaving Willow unable to follow. But he hadn't walked through walls in ages, at least not on purpose. And there was something about the rage in her hazel eyes, and the way her wild, copper hair seemed to churn like the turbulent waves of the sea, as though it was responding to her mood. She was a storm and the wind and the sunshine.

He couldn't take his eyes off her. So he let his back nudge the shelf and fancied himself in quite the compromising position. It was not entirely unpleasant.

"I have news for you, corpse boy," she said, pointing at his chest. "Women of my time are independent, have careers, own property, vote, even run for president. And we don't need a man to do it."

She was right up to his face now, and being at least half a foot taller than her, he grinned as he looked down upon her.

"You are quite the suffragette, Miss Ravensong. But you missed something in your research. The Moonstone was a safe haven for women activists. They congregated here and held meetings, and anyone who complained was shown the door."

Willow's mouth pressed shut with such ire, her bottom lip jutted into an adorable pout. So perfectly pink, those lips—pleasingly full and rounded with a cupid's bow. And also laced with venom.

Why did he find that so alluring? How could anything at all get a rise out of him? After all, he was not made of flesh and blood. However, feelings and emotions followed the soul into eternity. And right now, his feelings had a mind of their own.

He had never touched a woman in the heat of passion, nor did he consider force of any kind the gentleman thing to do. But Willow aroused a compulsion in his core, and he felt the overwhelming desire for human touch.

His fingers twitched at the shelf behind him until they found purchase on the spine of a book. Sliding it off the bookshelf, he lifted it so it was at Willow's shoulder height, holding it between them as both a barrier and form of contact. On the cover, a woman was engaged in a passionate embrace with what looked like a demon.

Apropos, he thought, considering Willow thought of him as a demon.

A little nudge of the book, and Willow's shoulder reeled. One more nudge, and she careened back.

"And another thing you're wrong about," he said, gently guiding her body to sway in a half circle so she was now back to the bookshelf. She let out a small gasp as she bumped against it—her palms spread out on the spines behind her. And if he didn't know better, he'd have sworn he saw sparks igniting at her fingertips. "A woman *does* need a man, just the same as a man needs a woman."

Montgomery shifted the book to press flat against Willow's chest applying the tiniest amount of pressure with his index finger, pitching her against the bookshelf. As he leaned in to whisper in her ear, her breath hitched deliciously, and a healthy bloom of strawberry spread across her cheeks.

"It is natural to need the opposite sex," he whispered against the shell of her ear. "It is natural to live in harmony with them. It is natural to love and to quarrel and to burn with desire. It is not weakness to give yourself fully to another. As long as there is friendship. As long as there is respect and mutual understanding."

She gulped audibly, practically heaving the words, "And... chemistry?"

Montgomery's gaze dipped to take in her features. Her flushed skin, her chin tipped back, and her mouth parted ever so slightly.

"Yes," he replied. "What I would give to have that opportunity again."

A wave of melancholy washed over him then, for he could not even say he'd loved and lost. Only lost.

Struck with cold awareness, he retreated from Willow's space, leaving her to clutch onto the book before it fell at her feet.

"Speaking of burning," he said soberly. "You better check on those cookies."

"You say witch
like it's a bad thing"

—Unknown

Chapter Nine

THERE IS A LIGHT
THAT NEVER GOES OUT

The darn purple box mocked Willow for the third time in as many days. To be fair, it wasn't the purple box itself, or even the discount Hobby Lobby crystal ball inside. It was her unalive roommate who was just moving things around now just to aggravate her.

After the encounter at the bookshelf, she couldn't maintain eye contact with Montgomery the rest of the day. That blasted bookcase caused her body to burn up just looking at it. She never did put that book back where he'd pulled it from the shelf. She'd clutched it to her chest while he left her standing there like a ninny.

Then, to get fresh air, she took her bike out for a spin around town. It wasn't until she'd gotten a few strange looks that she realized she'd been riding all over the place with *Ice Planet Barbarians* on full display in her bicycle basket.

She was too embarrassed to bring it back into the shop.

And even after the heated argument (and even more heated... whatever that was), the irksome ghost was still messing with her.

Just this morning, she couldn't find her shoes. When she pressed Montgomery about it, he flippantly pointed toward the storeroom, where Willow found the shoes in a box, along with a few other items she'd lost, like a hair claw and a remote control.

Then there was the pile of mail. After looking everywhere for it, she discovered the envelopes and papers filed away in several folders, each one with corresponding labels such as *'bills'* and *'banking'* etc. She had to admit the filing system made sense... for someone obsessive compulsive like Montgomery.

The purple box, however, did not make sense.

She certainly hadn't moved it, and since she hid it away after the first time she'd found it on top of a display table, she knew it wasn't a customer mindlessly picking it up and laying it down somewhere else.

"Dale?" she called across the shop. "Did you put this here?"

Willow was pleased with Dale's work so far. He caught on quickly, and really was good at upselling. Yeah, he was a little quirky, but so was she in her own way. It was a good fit, having him there.

He wandered over to Willow from behind the cash register slipping his man purse across his chest since it was almost quitting time. Apparently he had a hot date (his words), and spent the last five minutes dousing himself with cologne.

"Nope," he said, readjusting his sweater underneath the strap of his bag. "I wouldn't put that out. I have an aversion to purple."

"Hmmm, okay. May I ask why you don't like purple?"

"It just makes me very uncomfortable. Always has. You can ask Mother if you ever come to visit."

"I'll make a point of it," she replied.

Dale made his way to the front door, paused mid-stride, and pivoted around with his index finger up.

"I almost forgot. A package came for you while you were in the back. I put it behind the cash register."

"Thanks, Dale. Have a good night."

No sooner was he out the door, did Montgomery appear from wherever he was the past few hours. Sulking around creepily, no doubt.

"I thought he'd never leave," he said, taking it upon himself to turn all the locks.

"He left right on time," Willow said, throwing Montgomery a black look as she put the purple velvet box in a cabinet. "What do you care, anyway? You come and go as you please, no matter how many people are here."

"That is true. But you refuse to acknowledge me, and if I have something to say to you, I have to wait until the shop is closed."

Willow blew an exasperated sigh and glowered at him.

"Fine. What was so important you couldn't wait to say to me?"

"I'm going to need you to order *The Silmarillion*. I'm almost done with *Return of the King*, and—"

"Seriously? Are you even *trying* to remember what unfinished business you have here?"

"You don't know for certain that's why I'm here. Are you a ghost expert? Maybe this is it for me for all eternity." He shrugged with both shoulders, tossing his hands up.

"Why me?" Willow cried to the heavens. Then, picking up her phone, she tapped a few buttons and raised it to her ear."

"Who are you calling? Getting an update from your mother?"

"No. But that reminds me..."

She paused as the voice on the line answered the call in a mumbling, almost imperceivable drone. "Thank you for calling Szechuan Charlie's how can I help you?"

"Yes, I'd like to order a large Kung Pao chicken please."

"Take out or delivery?"

"Delivery."

Montgomery frowned. "You're trying to torment me, aren't you?"

"Oh, I can't decide. Let me ask my roommate." She half covered the phone with her hand and asked Montgomery, "Rice or noodles?"

"I see how you are," he said, shooting eye daggers at her.

"You're right," she replied, then returned to her phone call. "We'll have both."

She added cream cheese wontons and potstickers to her order, gave the Chinese restaurant worker her address and payment information, and after finishing the call, she reached down under the counter for the box Dale stored for her. There was no return address on the label, but Willow knew the signs it had been delivered by magic. It could only be from Esme.

Montgomery remained in place. Glowering at her.

"What?" she said with faux innocence. "You like Chinese food?"

"I've been to a few chop suey palaces in my time, yes."

"Then what's with the sour face? Oh that's right. You don't have a mouth."

"I have some semblance of a mouth, otherwise how could I be talking to you right now? I simply can't put anything in it."

"Believe me, if I could put something in your mouth to get you to stop talking, I would."

Willow's blush didn't overtake her until she noticed the repulsed horror in Montgomery's eyes even as his gaze dipped to her lips. Then, like a wave, heat bloomed in her cheeks, reaching the tips of her ears.

Do not think about the bookcase. Do not think about the bookcase.

"Anyway..." she said, forcing down a swallow. "We have a lot of work to do and it's going to be a long night. I have to eat."

Grateful for something to do with her hands, she reached for the scissors she kept on top of the register, but they weren't there.

"Where are my scissors, Boogie Man?"

"Top left drawer."

Willow glowered at him as she plucked the scissors from the drawer and sliced the package open at the seam. It was not a very large box, but there seemed no end to the items Esme had packed in there. A few divination candles, bundles of dried sage, a grimoire the size of the entire Encyclopedia Britannica, little jars of potions, crystals, charms, and a cauldron large enough for most witchy purposes.

"What, no dragon bones, Esme?" Willow joked under her breath as she arranged the objects side by side on the counter, tossing the box behind her.

"How did all those things fit in that little box?"

Willow shrugged. "Esme is really good at packing things."

"The book alone is an impossibility," he said incredulously.

"Says the ghost."

Montgomery pulled a face in disgust. "Are you... an occultist?"

"No!" Willow cried. "Of course not."

"Then what are those objects for?"

"Just a few things Esme thought would help you move on."

Montgomery stumbled a few steps back, making a cross with his two forefingers. "You're witches. It all makes sense now. The broom, the candles, how you open the trash bin with a wave of your hand..."

"The trash can has a battery operated motion sensor."

"You're a witch!"

"Oh relax. Only by blood. Okay wrong choice of words. Heritage. Only by heritage."

"Get back whence you came," he shouted with a wild look about him.

"That's rich coming from you, Ghostface. Anyway, I don't identify as a witch."

Montgomery, still crossing his fingers together, said tentatively, "If you don't identify as a witch, then how do you identify?"

"As a person. Now put your hands down and make yourself useful by drawing the blinds so passersby won't see me talking to myself."

After a moment of hesitation, Montgomery shuffled over to the windows and lowered them one by one, never taking his eyes off Willow. Once they were properly closed, he kept his distance from her, standing stiffly and cautiously.

"You're being ridiculous," Willow said. "Besides. I don't use my powers for anything. Not even a glamour charm."

She cracked open the grimoire, feathering through the ancient pages.

"I mean, what the heck is Putrefaction of Esoteric Rupture and where is someone supposed to find fillet of a fenny snake?"

She shook her head, already deciding this book would be of no use to her. But Montgomery did not appear convinced of it and kept a good distance away from her as though she was about to turn him into a toad.

"I have more faith in science than magic," she said warmly. "And I really believe if we could jog your memory somehow, we could fulfill whatever it is that needs to be done. And then you can finally rest in peace. We can talk it out and try to understand your unconscious feelings and thoughts. Like psychology."

Montgomery's posture relaxed a little, but he didn't respond. At length, Willow threw her hands up and started tossing the magical objects back into the box.

"You know what? Forget it."

"This," he said at last, gesturing toward the box, "is not something one easily forgets."

She sniffed, piling the objects on top of one another, unable to fit them back inside the box. "Sure. Over a hundred years to figure things out and *this* is what he remembers."

A knock on the door's window startled her, but it was only the food delivery.

Willow unlocked the door, thanked the delivery driver, took the bags back to the counter, unpacked all the food, and began eating... all in utter silence, as though Montgomery wasn't even there. For all intents and purposes, he really wasn't there. Physically at least. And ignoring his stares wasn't easy, what with those magnetizing eyes. But she didn't sign up for this, and she just wanted to move on with her life. And start planning that ball. And then maybe try to flirt with the cute diner owner, or someone else equally as nice. And alive.

After a long while, Montgomery said, "When you said you're a witch by heredity only, and that you don't identify with it, what did you mean?"

"First of all, I don't care for the word witch," she said with a mouthful of noodles. "All the negative connotations. Green skin. Warts and pointy hats. Plus, it rhymes with the 'b' word and I take great offense to that."

"But is it passed down? Like artistic talent? Or is it learned?"

"It's more like... in our DNA."

"What is... DNA?"

"Right. I forgot you wouldn't have heard of it in 1912. It's the stuff our bodies are made of, I guess. Genetic structure. Cells and stuff. Like it comes from your bloodline... if someone's Italian... or Japanese or whatever, and who they're related to."

"Oh. I understand now. And you are ashamed of your heritage?"

"No. Not ashamed, per se. I just... It's not *who* I am. I want to be so much more."

"Like what?"

"I don't know. I love books. I love *stories*. Books are a special kind of magic. They spark the imagination, take you to far away worlds, and they make you feel so many wonderful things. You know, they say someone who reads books lives a thousand lives, but someone who doesn't read, only lives one. I read that on an internet meme."

Montgomery only hummed in thought, turning his gaze to the side. After a short time, he spoke, but didn't look back at Willow.

"My father left when I was but two years old. I don't remember him, but Mother always said he was handsome." He snorted derisively at the thought. "She only ever had good things to say about him even after he'd abandoned us without a penny. He never deserved her praise." He lowered his gaze and his face grew cold as if the anger was washing over him anew. "He was Irish. My mother was Scandinavian, though she didn't talk about it much or share any family traditions with me. And when I was thirteen, she died."

"I'm sorry," Willow said softly. "How horrible it must have been, to be so young and alone."

"I made my way," he said in a hard tone. "I had a found

family. People I met through the years. Folks who stayed in my life, not because they had to. But because they wanted to."

He looked at Willow now, and had such an expression of misery, she couldn't help but feel a pang in her chest. As infuriating as he was in the afterlife, she had to admit, he was dealt a crappy hand while he was alive.

"So, yes," he continued. "I understand what it is to leave one's ancestry behind in order to move forward."

"Did you ever see your dad again? Maybe he's your unfinished business."

"He showed up here one day, after he'd learned of the saloon's success. Oh, he put on a good act, crying and repentant. Saying he'd turned over a new leaf. But what he really wanted was money."

"What a jerk."

"Quite right. When I caught him stealing, I threw him out and told him I never wanted to see him again. He's not my unfinished business, I can assure you."

"That really sucks," said Willow, and Montgomery cringed a little at her liberally modern vocabulary. But surely he'd be used to slang by now. He'd been around in the sixties, after all.

Willow returned to her Kung Pao chicken, but with such a heavy subject hanging in the air between them, she felt the need to clarify something.

"Witches aren't evil," she said. "Not any more evil than regular humans, anyway. It's not like we go around casting hexes on people. Magic is just a convenience, like when you can't be bothered to do laundry or put on makeup. And when we want to pretend we're Jedis."

She shrugged with amusement.

"Esme uses herbs for healing and some fun little spells. But nothing bad. Of course, just like everyone in the world, there *are* witches who are inherently bad. Just like not all Irishmen are bad just because your father was."

"You call your mother by her first name. Why?"

Willow blinked, never having thought of it before. "I dunno. She likes it that way. I think it makes her feel young. She does look more like she's my sister than a mom."

"My mother always seemed old," said Montgomery dolefully. "But she was only thirty-one when she passed. I remember her wrinkles and thinning hair. The harsh life she lived, I suppose."

"Tell me about your found family. Who were they?"

Willow had done as much research as she could, but there was no mention of a wife or children. But that didn't mean he didn't have a family. They didn't keep good records back in 1912—especially in small towns like Mysthaven, Connecticut.

Something in Montgomery brightened as he replied, like he was recounting his good days.

"The patrons of the bar were my people. My regulars. But also, friends.

We had a grand old time, me and the fellas. Walter, Roy, and Sam. What trouble we'd get into as boys. Harmless pranks, really. We'd put up fake signs on shop windows and such. As a youngster already working to support myself, I suppose it was a way to blow off some steam. I'm not terribly proud of my antics, but I have no regrets. We were inseparable, even as we became responsible adults. Walter married the girl next door, and Roy was a confirmed bachelor. And Sam. He was with me the day I opened the Moonstone."

He looked at Willow then. "I'm happy you kept the name."

"Sounds like a great bunch of guys," said Willow. "Maybe I can look them up to see what became of them. It might give us some clues."

"I'd appreciate that very much," said Montgomery. The last time I spoke to Sam, he'd met a young lady in New York. He was smitten. I wonder if he married her. Roy and I would jab fun at him for renouncing our bachelor pact..."

He trailed off, as if a new idea came into his head that took over all his other thoughts.

"By George, I remember something." His gaze swept to the bar and he pointed. "A woman."

"The woman from New York?"

"No," he said with a faraway look. "Someone else. She had... golden curls, and would sit alone, right over there. And she'd come in every night and smile and talk to me and..."

"And? What else?"

"Her face... streaked with tears. She was crying my name, bent over me as I lay on the floor. And then... the whole world faded away."

"OUR LITTLE LIFE
IS ROUNDED WITH A SLEEP."

-William Shakespeare

Chapter Ten

GHOST CODE

The memory came to him in short, quick flashes, much like the first moving pictures he'd seen as a lad. Montgomery stood perfectly still, closing his eyes to keep the vision from fading. To welcome more if it was indeed something of his past. But the memory was fleeting and was over almost as quickly as it began.

Who was that woman? And why could he not remember?

He was at the mouth of a tunnel, and the answers to all his questions were on the other side, waiting in the light. But nothing he did could bring him closer. He'd run, but the tunnel would stretch further and further away.

His whole existence was like that. Until recently. Until this tornado of a woman with fiery red hair moved into his bar. Now, everything shifted, and the world around him came into focus. Before, moments were spread out like a jigsaw puzzle, or as if his soul was meandering through a cloud, only partially aware. But slowly, day after day, time became linear, with a strange yet not unpleasant weight.

"Hello? Ghostface. What did you remember? Who was she?"

Willow was flapping her hands in front of Montgomery's face, her hazel eyes dancing with curiosity—and with a piece of noodle stuck to her chin. He blinked at the sight of her. So animated and lively... and a little odd. His fingers itched to wipe that noodle off her face, for his thumb to brush the remaining oils and sauce from her skin. Willow Ravensong was an enigma.

"I know why you can see me now," he said in a stupor. "It's your magic. Something about you is bringing my memories to light. It's because of you."

"Me? No, I'm nothing special."

"You can see me and talk to me because you're... well, I know you hate the word."

"A witch?"

"Yes," he replied tentatively.

"It's okay. You can say witch. The alternative is 'mage' or 'wizard' and that's just too *Harry Potter* for my taste."

"Alright then. And I'm sorry. I shouldn't have reacted the way I did. I know you can communicate with me because you're a witch. It's because of your magic—"

"I'm gonna stop you right there. Witches don't just see ghosts all over the place. You're thinking about mediums, and even they have to work for it. Besides, Esme and my sisters didn't see you when they came for the grand opening."

"There were a lot of people here. Maybe they thought I was one of the crowd. You said yourself I don't appear like a spirit. Even... I dare say... handsome?"

Willow opened her mouth then clamped it shut again, making a gurgling noise in the back of her throat. A soft bloom of pink spread across her features and she stuttered when she said, "Wha...? Handsome? Chaw! If pasty and gaunt is the new hot."

"Pasty and gaunt?"

She waved her finger up and down. "You look like death warmed over."

"Oh yeah? You look like..." Montgomery wasn't sure what she looked like, exactly. An intrepid sprite? A feral raccoon? A flighty fox? "...like you were raised by monkeys."

"How very original of you to say that," she said, planting her fists on her hips. Did you learn that in your misspent youth?"

"I was fully supporting myself at fourteen. At that age you were playing with dolls, no doubt."

"I don't know what you think American teenagers do in the twenty-first century, but it's not playing with dolls."

"Seeing as though you thrive in chaos, I wonder what you *did* do with your time."

Willow gasped dramatically. "You did not just go there."

Montgomery could only guess what she meant by *'go there'* but he knew he'd crossed some kind of line if her heated complexion offered any inclination.

At length, he let out a sigh and drifted to the bar to take a seat. The stools were covered in midnight blue velvet-like cushions and had brass arm rests. He could at least admit, reluctantly, that Willow had good taste in decor. He would have loved to afford such luxurious embellishments when he ran the Moonstone.

"I do not find joy in bickering with you, Miss Ravensong," he said at last. "In fact, I have not found joy in anything these past one hundred plus years. Death. The undiscovered country from whose bourn no traveler returns."

He hung his head over the bar and, after a length of silence, thought Willow had left the room. But then felt a quickening when he sensed her presence beside him.

"I suppose I can forgive a guy who quotes Shakespeare," she said, settling onto the next stool. "I mean, slapping you in the throat isn't an option, so..."

"The world has changed a great deal, has it not? It is quite jarring."

"Yes, it has. But you've seen it all take place, haven't you? You've haunted this place for over a hundred and ten years. It's like witnessing history firsthand. The world wars, the moon landing..."

"I do not experience time like the living," he said. "My consciousness fades in and out, like it's all a dream. Sometimes I find myself in a vast, dark room, other times it's like walking through fog. And when I'm present in the Moonstone, this dimension seems jumbled up... and there are pieces missing from one day to the next. I haven't had a full day of cognizance for over a century. Until recently, when you came."

"You don't remember all the ways this town has changed?"

"I remember some things. For a time, there was always music. Rock and roll, playing constantly." He shook his head.

"Back when this was a record store?"

"Yes."

Willow laughed. "And you hated rock and roll. You're such an old fogey."

"I don't hate rock and roll now," he said defensively. "It grew on me. There are quite a few artists I enjoy, actually."

"And then they opened the sports bar," she said. "Do you remember that?"

"Oh yes. The enormous food servings. And even bigger

electric telescopes—colorful and distracting—each one displaying a different sporting event. And the patrons shouting at the images on screen. The awareness of those times are few but there are some that stuck with me."

"Seems rowdy," said Willow, and Montgomery reflected on the soft jazz or classical music she liked to play when the bookshop was open.

He lifted his chin, fixating on a thought. "Can I ask you a question?"

"I guess."

"What does...a cheeseburger taste like?"

Willow let out a little chuckle and regarded him curiously. "Like a hamburger but with cheese."

He thought as much, but felt unsatisfied with the answer.

"The burgers they served in the sports bar looked quite a bit different than the hamburger steak sandwiches of my time."

"You think about food a lot, don't you?" she asked.

"Wouldn't you?" he replied, eyebrows raised.

Willow gave him a pitying look, and after a few moments of quiet thought, said, "Well, you aren't missing much."

Then she hopped off the stool, went over to the sales counter with a determined stride, and tossed her Chinese food in the trash.

"That's going to leave a smell," Montgomery said, even as Willow strode toward the back of the shop, waving him over to join her.

"Come on, Casper. I want to show you something."

He supposed he had nothing else to amuse him, so he followed and was surprised she was leading him upstairs. These quarters used to be where he kept his office, and he had a small bed in the corner where he'd sleep, hoping to save enough one day for a fine home. But that never happened.

Willow opened the door to her apartment and strode inside, expecting him to join her. But Montgomery only stood at the threshold, feeling a touch discomfited.

"What's wrong?" Willow asked when she looked back. "Will this doorway throw you back on your butt, too?"

"No it will not. But as this is now a woman's bedroom, I cannot enter."

"You can't? Is that some kind of ghost code? I gotta say that makes me kind of relieved that ghosts just can't watch people in the shower."

"It's not ghost code," he said unamused. "It is the virtue of a gentleman. I would never enter a woman's chambers in life, and will not start to do so in death."

Willow stared into the middle distance. "So... ghosts *can* watch people in the shower?"

"I imagine so."

"And they can write *'boo'* on bathroom mirrors?"

Montgomery sighed forcefully. "There was something you wanted to show me? Could you not show it to me downstairs?"

"I only have one TV and it's in here. Or as you like to

call it... electric telescope. Besides, we'll have Patrick Swayze as a chaperone."

Zephyr brushed past Montgomery at that point, looking back at him before pouncing on the bed, as if it were an invitation to enter the room.

"Are you quite sure you want me to come in?"

"I insist," Willow replied.

"I was talking to the cat."

Zephyr meowed at that, which seemed confirmation enough for Montgomery, so he took a few steps inside.

Willow chuckled. "He's just a regular cat. He doesn't understand you. Unless you say the word D-I-N-N-E-R. I'm still upset about that, by the way."

Montgomery looked around the room while Willow turned on the television, navigating to the streaming apps to find what she was looking for.

"Looks like I have to rent it," she said. "I should probably buy it at this point."

"What are you looking for?"

"*Ghost*. Now sit down, you can't watch the whole movie standing up." She patted the bed and clicked on the remote to order the movie.

"There are no chairs," he said. "And the bed is non-negotiable."

"Fine. I'll go get a chair from downstairs."

"No, no. Allow me."

"Wait. If you go downstairs, you'll change your mind and won't come back." She huffed, as though she was greatly inconvenienced, and finally nodded in resolution to whatever was going through her head. "Okay. Just hang on a second... and you might want to give me some space for your own safety."

She waved her arms in circles to shoo him to the corner, closed her eyes, and took a deep breath. Montgomery noted she was in the same stance as when she was trying to send him out of the building. But this time, a gust of air swept her hair from her neck, and a soft, blue light radiated from her fingertips. And right before his eyes, the shape of a chair began to appear in front of her, starting out as the same blue light from her hands, but then forming into something solid, until she closed her hands into fists and let out a long exhale.

She opened one eye, and then the other, and seemed pleased to see what she had done. Then she looked at Montgomery in amazement.

"I did it. And without sending us into a black hole."

Montgomery hoped she was joking, not very fond of black holes or anything else as equally ominous. And he should have been amazed by the magic he'd just witnessed. A chair Willow conjured out of thin air was nothing to shake a stick at. But he just looked at it with a puzzled brow, inclining his head to one side.

"Are there supposed to be only three legs?" he asked.

Willow grimaced. "Not ideally."

"No bother," he replied cheerfully. "I'll make due."

In theory, it shouldn't have mattered. Montgomery was, after all, weightless. But the laws of physics tended to elude him. And even though a living human wouldn't fall off a three-legged chair if they sat correctly, this chair wouldn't abide by such bothersome rules. Perhaps because it was made with magic. But when he sat down, it wobbled under him, tipping him over onto the floor.

"I'm sorry, Montgomery," Willow said in earnest. "This is one of the reasons I don't do magic."

"It's perfectly alright," he said. "I'll be fine on the floor. And... my friends call me Monty."

"I'm your friend?" she asked nonplused.

"You'll do," he replied, and allowed a crack in his smile.

"Okay," she said, tossing him a pillow. "Monty."

She made herself comfortable on her bed, petting her cat, and played the movie, pretty much talking the entire time. Every now and then she'd glance over to Montgomery, asking if certain scenes triggered him, or if anything he saw helped him in any way. He told her he wasn't bothered in the slightest, although there were a couple moments that sent his heart racing—particularly the pottery wheel scene.

Eventually, he picked himself off the floor to recline on the bed, but kept a good distance between himself and Willow.

It was a silly thing, he knew it. He was no longer flesh and bone, and he would remove himself from her room as soon as the movie ended. But Willow set him at ease with the way she hummed and laughed at the screen, and the soft way she'd talk throughout the film, telling him she'd

be there to listen once he decided to tell her if he remembered anything else, or who the blonde woman was.

But he didn't know. And right now, he didn't care. He
suddenly felt more at peace than he had in life or death.
And for the first time in one hundred and eleven years, he
closed his eyes, and let sleep overtake him.

"Some people are born for Halloween, and some are just counting the days until Christmas."

-Stephen Graham Jones

Chapter Eleven

WHO IN THE WORLD IS
TIMOTHEE SHABLAGOO?

He looked so peaceful that she didn't want to wake him. Then again, how could she wake someone up who wasn't even alive? Hadn't he mentioned he never slept? Willow supposed if she hadn't slept in over a century, she'd be pretty frickin' tired, too.

So she left him alone, settling on the mattress beside him. Watching him. How was he so beautiful? She'd thought she found him so striking because of those unreal green eyes, the way they seemed to stare deep into her soul. But now, with his lashes fanned over his pearlescent cheeks, and a straight, celestial nose leading a path from perfectly symmetrical brows to his tidy mustache, she was convinced Montgomery Harland was as lovely as he was perplexing.

She fell asleep next to him, and dreamt again of balls and lavish gowns, but this time it was 1912 fashion and she was dressed like Jane Seymour in *Somewhere in Time*, and Montgomery was Christopher Reeve. When she awoke, he was no longer in her bed, and she didn't see him before she left for her morning errands.

There was a Women's Business Council meeting in an hour, and she rode her bicycle to Bo's Diner on the way. That copy of *Ice Planet Barbarians* was still in the basket.

Bo seemed ecstatic to see her, and although the diner seemed extra busy, he had her pumpkin pancakes with cinnamon butter ready before her coffee was cool enough to sip.

"I picked up the property records for your shop," he said, barely slowing down on his way to refill someone's coffee. "But they're at my house. If I'd known you were coming in today..."

"That's okay. I can pick them up another time."

"I can bring them to you," said Dale, who was having his breakfast next to her at the counter. "I know where Bo lives."

"Or I can bring them to your bookshop myself," Bo said, giving Dale the side eye.

"Either works fine for me," said Willow.

An older man sitting at a window table waved his empty coffee cup in the air. "Excuse me!"

Bo grunted with an infinitesimal roll of the eyes.

"I'll be right back." He gave Dale a look and walked off.

"What's that look for?" Willow asked.

Dale, still with a bite of waffle in his mouth, replied, "He's sweet on you."

"Oh!"

"Don't worry. He's too shy to act on it. He just wants to make sure I don't either."

Willow chanced a puzzled glance over her shoulder at Bo. "He doesn't strike me as the shy type."

"Only when it comes to women. He had a tough breakup a few years ago, and personally, I don't think he ever got over it."

"That's too bad," Willow said thoughtfully. "And what about you? How did your hot date go?"

"It went fine. I thought I might end the date by taking her back to my place for some Studio Ghibli trivia, but Mother was already asleep."

"That's a shame. So... any fun plans for Halloween?"

He gave her a serious look. "Nah. Mysthaven isn't a place you want to be out in on Halloween. This town may seem like the perfect setting for a Hallmark movie, but there's a seedy underbelly."

"Really? But isn't the Harvest Festival a family friendly wholesome good time?"

"On the surface, maybe. But once the sun goes down, there's an otherworldly presence in the air." He leaned in closer to her to whisper, "And legend has it there are witches living in the Cinnamon Woods."

"Stop weaving your spooky tales," Bo said, returning just in time to hear the last part of the conversation. "There are no witches in the Cinnamon Woods or anywhere else in Mysthaven. Witches aren't real. Don't believe a word he says, Willow. Would you like more coffee?"

"I'm good, thanks. But let's say for the sake of argument, witches were real. Why would they live in the woods? Wouldn't they prefer a nice apartment in town? They could magic up a beautiful mansion, probably."

Most witches lived comfortable but unassuming lives, not wanting to bring too much attention to themselves by owning extravagant homes and cars. But there were a few outliers. Those were the ones who played around with the stock market, and they didn't live in places like Mysthaven or Crescent Hollow.

"I don't know why they live in the woods," Dale said. "But sometimes when there's a full moon, strange things happen."

"There's a full moon this Halloween," Bo said. "I think it's kind of romantic." He chanced a quick glance at Willow, then bowed his head to wipe up the already clean counter.

Willow thought his bashful side was kind of cute. Surely he was a nice guy. Why shouldn't she like him? After all—he had the most important attribute going for him, which was that he was alive.

"Not only is it a full moon," added Dale. "It's an extremely rare super blue blood moon. That's why I'll be playing my bagpipe that night. Did you know that the bagpipe wards off bad omens?"

"Speaking of bad omens," Willow said, remembering the last time she walked home from Bo's Diner, "Do you guys know everyone in this town?"

"I'd say about seventy-five percent of Mysthaven residents eat here on a regular basis," Bo replied. "Why?"

"It's just that, the other day, a young man kind of startled me. He was coming out of Tom's Market as I was walking down the sidewalk. I dunno, he was probably harmless, but I got the heebie jeebies."

"What did he look like?" Dale asked.

"Tall and thin. Something about him reminded me of that actor in Dune. I can never pronounce his name."

"Sting?" Bo guessed.

"No. The newer movie. Timotay Charcuterie... or Chardonnay."

"Timothée Chalamet?" supplied Dale.

"Yes, exactly. Do you know him?"

"No. I don't know a lot of celebrities," answered Dale. "But I did meet Jennifer Lopez once. Well, not so much as met her, really. She smiled at me as she passed by with her entourage. It was in New York, not here in Mysthaven."

"That's fascinating, Dale," Willow said. "But I meant do you know who the guy is that *looks* like Timothée Shablagoo?"

"Not a clue."

"Me neither," Bo said.

"How do you know it wasn't the real Timothée Chalamet?" asked Dale in all seriousness.

"Well, if I see him again, I'll ask him if he is," Willow replied cheerily. She wasn't going to let it bother her any more.

"Say, I might be a tiny bit late to the shop today," she said after a moment. "I have a Women's Business Council meeting and it might go long. You don't mind?"

Bo grunted derisively and slapped the towel over his shoulder.

"I've got you covered," Dale said. "Should I put out the cookies?"

Willow wasn't sure how comfortable she was with Dale going into the kitchen while she wasn't there to make sure no plates were floating unexplainably.

"No thanks. I'll take care of it when I get there."

"I'll get your papers to you as soon as I can," said Bo before shouting over her head, "Your Denver omelet is coming, lady. This ain't Denny's."

Then he gave Willow an apologetic grimace. "I better quit yappin' so these people can eat and get outta my diner."

Willow only smiled at him, but inside she mused how

Bo would make an even grumpier ghost than Montgomery. He'd be the kind to throw plates.

After her meal, she biked over to Nadine's house for the Women's Business Council meeting.

The same luxury cars sat in the driveway, but this time, she was a little less impressed, and a little more indifferent.

The other members were already there, making her wonder if they always showed up extra early. Rowena had brought cranberry brie puff pastry tarts, and Jewels thought it was appropriate to bring champagne for no other reason than it was probably happy hour in Paris. Willow didn't care to do the math on that one.

"I don't think you told me what kind of work you're in, Jewels," Willow said, sipping from her glass. It was pretty good champagne.

"I'm a travel agent," Jewels answered with no further explanation before taking a giant bite of pastry.

"That's cool," Willow replied warmly, although a little confused. "I didn't realize people still used travel agents."

"Oh, it's a huge industry. I cater to corporations and filthy rich people who can't be bothered to book their own travel."

"Everyone knows, if you want a penthouse suite with a view, you call Jewels," Astrid said.

"Jewels got each of us our own over-water bungalows in Bora Bora for my birthday," added Daria. "Maybe you'd like to join us for our next jaunt."

"That sounds amazing," Willow said. She was beginning to appreciate the perks of signing up for the Women's Business Council membership. Esme always said it pays to know the right people.

"Now, on to our first order of business," Nadine announced. "Willow, I told the others before you arrived —we're getting together here at my house before the Harvest Festival. We'll meet right before sunset to give us plenty of time. And don't worry about your booth. Everything will be set up for you."

"Okay," Willow agreed. "I was already planning on closing the shop early."

"You might consider not opening at all that day," Nadine said. "Nobody shops on Halloween. Oh, and unfortunately, I'll have to ask you to come alone. What happens in the MWBC stays in the MWBC."

"MWBC?"

Astrid explained. "Mysthaven Women's Business Council, dear."

"It's just that I have gifts for you all, and we're a tight knit group," Nadine said. "Just in case you were thinking of bringing the young man who works for you."

"Oh no, he wouldn't want to come," said Willow. "I'll be flying solo. Well, not literally flying, obviously."

No broom travel Willow, thank you very much.

"Alright. That's good," said Nadine. "How is business going for you so far?"

"Oh, it's amazing. A few hiccups, but nothing I can't handle."

"What kind of hiccups?" Rowena questioned.

A ghost, for one thing. But Willow didn't want that morsel of information to get around.

"Just me, trying to get my sea legs. I was thinking of throwing a costume ball. Just a small one if I can get around to planning it."

"That sounds lovely," Daria said. "You'll invite all of us, right?"

"You'll be first on the guest list," Willow said cheerily.

"Wonderful," Jewels exclaimed. "I'll watch for my invitation. More champagne?"

"Actually," Willow replied, "I drank too much coffee this morning. May I use the bathroom?"

"Of course," said Nadine, shifting her eyes to signal Astrid who rose from her seat right away.

"I'll show you where it is," Astrid said, and led Willow out of the room, and down a hallway. When they reached a plain, white door, she proclaimed, "Here you go. I'll wait right here. Turns out, I have to go, too."

Willow guessed from the way the modern fixtures looked so different from the rest of the vintage house, that this was where the guests used the facilities, and she was okay with that. She once used the toilet in an old house that had the water tank hanging from the ceiling. She didn't think she'd pulled the chain very hard, but ended up flooding the whole bathroom. Thank the Fates Nadine had a nice guest restroom. There was even a basket of cute monogrammed hand towels for single use.

When Willow was done with her business, Astrid asked her to wait so they could walk back together. So she passed the time enjoying the artwork on the walls and the photographs of Nadine and what looked like old family photos. Some were black and white or sepia, and a few others looked like studio portraits. But one photo in particular stole her breath right from her lungs.

It was of a young man with a thin, pale face, and unruly black hair. The Timothée Chipotle look-alike.

"THE FIRST TIME
I CALLED MYSELF A 'WITCH'
WAS THE MOST MAGICAL
MOMENT OF MY LIFE."

-Margot Adler

Chapter Twelve

THERE MUST BE MORE THAN THIS PROVINCIAL LIFE!

T he haze lifted and Montgomery found himself once again in familiar surroundings. The last thing he remembered was drifting off while watching a movie. And he'd been on Willow's bed of all places. He didn't know how much time had passed since then. Sleep in the conventional sense was not his companion. There was no rest in the afterlife. No closing one's eyes to slumber in sweet dreams. No waking up with the sun, refreshed and ready for the day.

Only a spectral flicker in and out of consciousness, like a leaf drifting on a gust of wind. For a century he existed this way, wandering between the living realm and an empty nothingness as if walking from one room to another—sometimes noticing weeks, months or even years had passed.

But this time was different. He felt a breeze against his cheek, the warmth of the sun on his skin, and could smell the freshness in the air. Freshly cut grass. Fragrant pine. The clear running water of a mountain stream. Birds chirping in the distance. And while he was in that place, he sensed a coaxing, as if he could make the decision to stay or return.

It was his hesitation which sent him gently back until he was standing in the middle of the bookshop, observing Willow on the floor mumbling jumbled words over her ancient book.

Then, as if sensing him there, she paused, sat up stone still, and said curtly, "Where have you been?"

He wasn't exactly sure where he'd been. Only that it had never happened that way before.

Willow slowly stood up from the floor, where Montgomery now noticed was littered with candles and gemstones, and turned to face him with seething fury. Her skin seemed to glitter. Her eyes like hot coals. And her hair —as wild and torrid as the surface of the sun—danced like tattered staysails in a tempest.

"Three days, Montgomery. Three. Freaking. Days. I was worried sick about you."

"Three days?"

"I didn't know where you'd gone—if you were gone forever or not. If you finally found a way to leave the building. If you just ceased to exist. If I'd made the whole thing up in my head and would have to be institutionalized..."

"And you were worried about me?"

"I thought maybe watching *Ghost* helped you move on, like gave you some ideas. I dunno! And it freaked me out."

"But why? I thought you wanted me gone."

"I... do!" she said with a hint of hesitation. "Totally. But I want to see it with my own eyes just to make sure you won't come back."

"What on earth did you think it would look like?"

She threw her hands into the air. "A... bright white light summoning you to walk into it?"

"A bright white light?"

"Sure."

"What if it's the other place?"

"Then a dark, scary shadow. What do I care?"

"You care," he said in wonder. "You missed me."

"I did not."

He gestured to the grimoire and witchy paraphernalia on the floor. "You missed me and you were trying to bring me back."

She scoffed. "Ha! As if."

Something within him swelled beyond comprehension, and he felt the overwhelming compulsion to gather Willow in his arms to steady the storm around her. It was then that he noticed her puffy eyes and the tears clinging to her lashes.

"Willow... have you been crying?"

"No!" she snapped, even as tears welled up anew. "I'm just pissed off."

She doused out her candles with a swift wave and swished her hands in a spiral until the gemstones rose on their own, caught up in the tornado of her magic. Her arms swept in circles above her head, sending the objects to fly around the room, all while streams of tears tracked down her cheeks.

"How dare you take off for days, leaving me to wonder what happened to you?"

She sliced an arm to her right, sending gemstones to a small box. Not all of them found their way inside, a few rebounding across the shop.

"You lied when said you couldn't leave. Was that flying backwards stint all for show?"

She flexed her fingers until they bunched into angry fists, obliterating the candles into a fine dust.

"Whoa, easy now," Montgomery said, holding up his hands. "We can talk about this."

"I don't want to talk about it. I want to hate you."

"No you don't."

"I do. I absolutely do. Should I count the ways? Let's see if I have enough fingers. One." She flicked her index finger, and a metal tumbler tipped over on the bar. "You use my witchy broom to sweep the floor." She ticked another finger up, this time causing a picture frame to wobble.

"Uh... Willow?"

"Two. You rearranged the travel books by color."

Another finger. "Three. You're just plain obnoxious."

A book flew off the shelf. Montgomery sensed her anger rising by degrees, consequently stirring a torrent of anger magic.

She continued to tick her fingers one by one, and as the numbers rose, so did her distemper.

Every flick of her wrist, every wild wave of her arm sent something flying or tumbling to crashing down. With each step, each rise in her ire, her surroundings responded like bits of papers caught in a whirlwind.

Her face was completely flush now, and despite it all, Montgomery thought she was radiant.

Her voice grew hoarse, raw from crying and speaking in a kind of feral growl. "You're insufferable," she cried as she started counting fingers on her second hand. "Disruptive. Maddening..."

Then, fully committed, she put her whole body into it and screamed, "Infuriating!"

With that, the entire top shelf of her highest bookcase spilled the books onto the floor. The noise was akin to a roof caving in. Or maybe it was just amplified by the magic.

Willow huffed and stomped over to pick up the books, mumbling about having to open the shop soon.

"Here, let me help you," Montgomery offered, but she snapped at him.

"I got this."

She picked up a few books, attempting to replace them on the shelves, but it was too high for her. Even jumping up on her tippy toes didn't help.

Frustrated, she grumbled, "I just want a rolling ladder like in Beauty and the Beast. Is that too much to ask?"

"Let me help you," Montgomery pleaded. But Willow waved him off, stomping across the aisle to get a step ladder.

"I'm perfectly capable alone, thank you. I can't expect you to stick around forever."

"Stubborn woman," thought Montgomery, watching her drag the step stool across the floor and ascending it with an armful of books. "Careful," he said with the smallest tug of foreboding.

Full of indignation, Willow paid no attention to Montgomery. In fact she was so miffed, her overconfidence and ambition to prove her point blundered her steps (as it often does when one is angry) and she lost her footing. The books fell first, crashing to the floor, most likely bending the pages and cracking the spines to the horror of book lovers everywhere. Then Willow flapped her arms in big circles as if she were doing the backstroke but without water.

Montgomery didn't consider how Willow might use magic to soften her fall, but in moments like these, one doesn't stop to think. Only react.

He'd never moved faster in his life (or death for that matter) and out of pure instinct, ran as Willow lurched backward, reaching out to save her from hitting the floor. She landed squarely in his arms, but as he didn't have the strength to hold her, he tumbled down, cradling her against his chest to cushion her fall.

She blinked as she looked up at his face, nestled like a baby in his embrace.

"You caught me," she said in a daze.

"I did," he replied. And in that moment, Montgomery forgot all about the argument, and that a hardcover was poking into his backside. All he saw was her. Those soft, hazel eyes still rimmed with pink, gazing at him with wonder. How her brows bunched together as her lips parted. How he could hold her like this forever and not be cross about it.

"This is why I don't do magic," she admitted.

"It's okay," he said softly. "Please know, I didn't leave on my own accord. I would have infinitely preferred to stay with you."

The softest blush bloomed across her features, and Montgomery decided he'd never seen anything more becoming, or more the subject of his desire. If he could only press his lips against hers and taste her kiss, he'd never want for anything.

"Monty?" Willow whispered.

"Yes, Willow?"

"You caught me."

His heart thundered with expectation.

"Yes," he said, fixated on her lips.

"No. You *caught* me."

She slipped her hand through his arms and touched his chest, pressing on it three or four times to test his density. Then, letting her hand wander up, cupped her palm on his jaw.

"How?"

A breath caught in Montgomery's throat just then as a stark realization crashed over him. He'd caught her, and now was holding her in his arms. Arms very much resembling solid, living arms made of flesh and bone and sinew.

Removing one arm from beneath her shoulder, he gently placed his hand over hers, inclining his head into it and closed his eyes.

"How indeed?" he said, overcome with emotion he couldn't describe. He wanted to cry but no tears came. He wanted to laugh, but no sound reached his throat.

"What is happening right now, Monty?"

"I don't know," he said. "Are you scared? Because I think I am."

He opened his eyes then, searching hers for answers, or maybe comfort. He only knew one thing. Willow Ravensong pulled him from the darkness. She was his bright white light.

At once her body tightened under his touch and her eyes darted toward the front door.

"Do you hear that?" She turned her gaze back at Montgomery and froze in panic. "Keys. It's Dale."

Wiggling out of Montgomery's arms, she shot to her feet just as the front door opened.

"Hi Dale," Willow chirped. "You're early."

"No I'm not," he replied. "I'm right on time. What happened in here?"

"Oh just doing some... rearranging."

"This place is a mess!"

"Don't worry. I have a system. Do you want to go over to Bo's to grab us some coffee?"

"I already did. And I picked up those property records while I was there."

Montgomery peeled himself off the floor, feeling every prickle of discomfort in his body. He never imagined pain would give him so much joy.

As he stood, emerging from behind one of the bar height bookshelves, he stayed a few feet behind Willow as she spoke to Dale, making an effort to remain quiet. But something strange happened. Dale's eyes shifted, and he stared right at Montgomery.

"Who's that?" Dale questioned suspiciously.

"Who's who?"

Montgomery wondered if Willow was testing Dale or trying to buy time. It was a delicate situation which was too new. If Dale could indeed see him, how did he appear to him? Like a spirit? Like a man?

But Dale pointed right at Montgomery. "Him. Did you hire another employee? Because you said you couldn't afford more hours and we have an agreement. I can't give up any of my hours."

"He's not an employee," Willow said defensively.

"Oh." Then Dale tipped his chin at Montgomery in greeting. "Sup."

Montgomery nodded back to him in turn.

"Are you Willow's boyfriend?" Dale asked.

"Yes!" blurted Willow. Exactly that. "My boyfriend. Mo... Mon... Mountie. She shuffled back a few steps, hooking her arm in Montgomery's. "Mountie, this is Dale. My sales clerk."

"Mountie's an interesting name," Dale said. "Is it Arabic?"

"Canadian," Willow said immediately. "He... was named after the Mountie Police. His parents were big fans of those wide brimmed hats."

Dale nodded, completely buying it. "I had a Canadian girlfriend once. Nobody believed me, though. Eventually we broke up."

"Um... did you say something about property records?" Willow said to redirect the conversation before she got in too deep with the lie.

"Yes, they're right here," Dale replied, retrieving a manila envelope from his messenger bag. "Bo said he sweet talked Mrs. Johnson into including the change of ownership statements."

"That's real nice of Bo," said Willow.

Dale nodded solemnly. "Yeah. He'll be a little gloomy when he finds out you have a boyfriend."

"I'm sure he'll be fine," said Willow, and something clenched inside Montgomery's stomach.

Dale stood in awkward silence, looking from Willow to Montgomery to the mess of books all over the shop, just taking it all in like it was the most natural thing in the world.

Then clapping his hands together said, "Okay well, I'll head to the office to clock in and check my socials. I posted a video of me juggling tiny pumpkins and I think it's about to go viral."

With that, he pranced into the back office, leaving Montgomery and Willow to process what just happened.

"Oh my lanta! He can see you." Willow squealed.

Montgomery, regarded her coolly. "Mountie? Really?"

"I panicked. I didn't want him to put two and two together and find out you're a ghost."

"Somehow I don't think he'll make that connection," said Montgomery. "He's too busy juggling pumpkins and playing the bagpipes."

"He brought over the property records with change of ownership statements. Your name is at the top of that list."

"He didn't read it. And now he thinks we're in a romantic relationship. And who is Bo?"

"Are we going to address the elephant in the room AKA you standing here in the flesh?"

"It's not fully processed yet. Ooh! I forgot what a headache feels like." Montgomery clutched his head and leaned onto the bookshelf. "I need a minute."

He felt like he was experiencing all his senses at once, and it was both thrilling and nauseating.

"You know what I find interesting?" Dale announced as he re-entered the room. He was brushing his teeth, holding his end of the conversation while attempting to keep toothpaste in his mouth. "Every single one of the owners of this building died a mysterious death."

"You looked at the records?" Montgomery asked.

"What else was I supposed to do while eating breakfast?"

Willow shot Montgomery a smug *'told you so'* look while Dale went behind the bar to spit in the sink.

"This is all getting weirder and weirder," Willow whispered to Montgomery. I still need to tell you about Talon Bickford."

She waited for Dale to amble back into the office, then told Montgomery about the young man who accosted her with the ominous message.

"At first I thought he was just a weird guy, but the more I thought about it, the more I wondered if he knew this place was haunted. And then I find out he's Nadine's son. The one who didn't want to work here. Now I'm thinking he's superstitious about the previous owners' deaths."

"What kind of name is Talon Bickford?"

"Never mind that. Focus. He knows something we don't know. We need to find him."

All this was disturbing and interesting to Montgomery seeing as he still couldn't remember how he died. He doubted the records Dale brought over had any more insight into the cause of his death than Willow's research she did on that thing she called the internet. No one was more invested than him. But in this moment a hollow pang tunneled through his core and he wondered if it was causing his headache and the feeling of vertigo that rushed over him suddenly. He reeled a little and Willow flew to him.

"Are you okay?" she asked with grave concern.

He regarded her lovely features and wondered if she had something to do with the choice he was given. Was he somehow here for her or was there some grander plan?

She smiled softly, and Montgomery decided then and there that she was made of stars. A glorious phenomenon of glittering light. And the most spectacular, shining part of her was her soul.

But he couldn't say such a thing to a woman, especially right after coming back to life after being dead for a hundred and eleven years.

And besides, he had more immediate matters to address. First of which was a biological necessity.

"Willow, my dear," he said. "I do believe I'm hungry."

"DON'T HAVE A CUP OF COFFEE
THIS HALLOWEEN.
HAVE A CAULDRON OF COFFEE INSTEAD."

-Anthony T. Hincks

Chapter Thirteen

SECOND BREAKFAST

The man ate like a Hobbit. Willow had never seen someone eat so much in her life. Then again, she supposed one would build up quite the appetite after one hundred and eleven years. After only twenty-four hours, Montgomery devoured every morsel of food in her kitchen. She even made extra batches of cookies and muffins. Where did he put it all?

When Montgomery polished off the last egg first thing in the morning and then announced he was still hungry, Willow said, "We're going to have to eat out today. I don't think I can keep up."

"Out?" he said with worry in his brow. "No, it would be best if you went to the market. Can you pick up a ham while you're there?"

"It's Sunday. And on Sundays, I don't cook or work. It's my only day off."

"So, you will order on the phone? Like you did when the Chinese food came?"

"No. I need to get out of this place for a while. And I think we should probably take you shopping for some new clothes."

"You do remember what happened last time I tried to walk through that door."

"That was before you grew a whole body."

"We don't know the rules. I could get thrown into another dimension."

They had spent the entire evening puzzling over the miracle of Montgomery's corporal awakening and came up blank. Willow even chanced conjuring a mirror charm to contact Esme for help. She did not crack the mirror, and there was no black smoke, thank the Fates. And of course her sisters Ivy and Bliss ran to the mirror to take a peek behind Esme's shoulders at the man who might or not be still a ghost. It was quite thrilling and perplexing to all four of the witches, but no matter how many books they searched through that night, there was no indication something like this had ever happened before. They ended the night more confused than ever, and Esme made Willow promise she'd bring her ghostman to visit.

"We're exploring new territory here. Anything can happen at any time." Willow wrapped her hand around Montgomery's and squeezed. "I'll go through the door with you and I promise I'll hold on tight."

Montgomery squeezed back. "Don't let go."

"I won't let go."

Willow stood up taking Montgomery with her and walked right up to the front door. "Ready?"

"Not even a little bit."

"No time like the present. On three. One, two... oh wait. I almost forgot my purse." She let go of him momentarily, leaving him at the door clutching his chest.

"The property records said I died of consumption? Are you sure it wasn't angina?"

"Just breathe. And close your eyes." Willow took his hand again and led him to the threshold, edging the tips of their toes right up to the doorway.

"I gotcha, boo," said Willow, and for good luck, she raised up on her tippy toes and kissed him on the cheek.

His surprise and delight set him in a blissful daze when Willow leapt through the door, pulling him along with her. When Montgomery's feet landed on the sidewalk, his whole face cracked into the widest smile Willow had ever seen. He puffed up his chest, lifted his face to the sun, and inhaled the first fresh air he'd breathed in over a century.

"You're still here," Willow said brightly, not letting go of him. But Montgomery tugged her by their adjoining hands and pulled her into his arms... and held on.

"Thank you," he whispered into her hair. And she sensed his voice quiver as he repeated again and again, "Thank you. Thank you."

When he pulled back, she watched a single tear track down his cheek and caught it with her thumb.

"See?" she said, showing him the drop on her thumb. "You drank so much tea, it's coming out of your eyeballs."

He sniffled and laughed mildly. "That reminds me. We're out of chamomile."

"We'll pick some up. But first, I want to take you somewhere."

They strolled down the sidewalk hand in hand (mostly because Montgomery wasn't sure if he'd disappear if he let go) and Willow watched him take in the modern updates to the town. He looked at everything in wonder, seeing many things for the first time.

"Goodness gracious," he said, "Look at these automobiles!"

"You haven't seen a modern car before?"

"On the television, yes. When the Moonstone was a sports bar. But never in person."

"What about the cars driving by the shop?"

"I could only see a few feet beyond the windows."

"Do you want to touch one?"

"Heavens no. I mean, yes... but I wouldn't dare."

"Why not?" Willow dragged him to the curb where an old, rusty economy car was parked. "Go ahead. Touch it."

She tapped her fingers on the hood to demonstrate.

"Will the owner be upset?" he asked.

Her top lip twitched as she side-eyed the car. "I'm pretty sure the owner would pay you to take it away."

With a measure of trepidation, Montgomery extended his hand and gingerly ran his palm over the front fender.

"Simply exquisite."

"Yeah. It's the epitome of luxury," she deadpanned. "Let's move on."

The short walk brought more gasps and gaping looks from Montgomery until they arrived at Bo's Diner.

"None of this was here before," he said in wonder. "It's the strangest feeling. Makes me a little sad."

"Lucky for you the cure for sadness is just through those doors. I am going to treat you to the best thing you've ever tasted."

As they walked in, Willow realized she'd only ever sat at the counter when she ate at Bo's. She felt a little weird sitting at one of the tables, especially with a man who was dead not very long ago. She still wasn't sure if he was still dead... or maybe undead. The whole business was a little hazy.

Bo approached their table almost immediately, handing them each a plastic-covered menu. He gave Montgomery a once-over and stood over him in his lumberjack way. "So, you're the boyfriend."

Montgomery stared back, his mustache twitching.

Willow jumped in before the two started a cockfight. "Bo, this is Mountie. He's visiting from..."

"Canada. I heard." Then Bo shifted his gaze to Willow and softened a bit. "I'm sorry it took so long to get the papers to you. I'm swamped from five in the morning 'til ten at night."

"It's fine, really," Willow said. "The bookshop's been keeping me busy, too."

"What kind of work are *you* in?" Bo asked Montgomery with a little edge in his questioning.

"I... it's a dying profession."

"Oh I get it," Bo said. "Dead end job?"

"Something like that."

Willow's efforts to hold in a laugh turned her face red.

Bo, too busy for puns, took out his notepad and poised his pencil.

"So, can I get you some pancakes?" he asked.

"Actually, we'll have two Bo burgers with bacon, extra cheese," Willow chirped.

"For breakfast?"

"Why not?" she replied. "Dale is always telling me how good they are."

Bo shrugged, having fulfilled stranger requests at all hours of the day. "Okay then. Fries or onion rings?"

"Both," Montgomery answered immediately. "I've wanted to taste onion rings for decades."

"You've never tried onion rings?" Bo asked in astonishment.

"The onion rings in Canada are different," Willow

explained. "All covered in gravy."

"If you say so," Bo replied, then triggered by the kitchen window bell, he yelled, "I'll be right there, Jose."

"And a couple of Cokes," Willow snuck in before Bo stormed back behind the counter. Then when he got to the window, Willow heard him say to the cook, "It's not *getting* cold, Jose. It's a parfait. It's already cold!"

"He's a charming fellow," Montgomery quipped.

"He's an acquired taste," Willow replied, to which Montgomery sniffed derisively. He looked around the diner fascinated, yet overcome by so much stimuli. He was a potential loose cannon, and Willow sensed he needed to narrow his focus on her, or he might break down in shock.

"Is this too much for you?" she asked, taking his hands in hers. He cast his eyes down on them and took a breath.

"I'm fine. I just feel like I'm in a completely different world. Not Mysthaven."

"Well, hey. Who knew you were so quick with the death puns?"

"I have no idea what you're talking about."

"In this century we call them Dad Jokes."

"Why?"

"Because they're so bad, they're funny."

Montgomery shook his head. "I'm sure there are a great many things I will never understand about your generation, least of all your sense of humor."

"That reminds me of something I wanted to talk to you about. I'd like to throw a ball, but I don't know if I can plan something before Halloween."

Originally, she had her heart set on the Regency era, but now, after that Somewhere in Time dream, she decided the theme should be 1912.

"When is Halloween?" Montgomery asked. "I've lost track of time."

"In about ten days, which gives me a week to prepare. But I wouldn't be able to pull it off without some..." She leaned in to whisper. "Magical intervention."

"Don't look at me. I can't even spook anymore."

"I'd just like to know if you'd oppose. Try to burn me at the stake or throw me in the river to see if I float."

He clenched her hands. "I know I first overreacted when I found out about your... heritage. But I wouldn't be here if it weren't for your talents. You are a gifted individual and shouldn't be ashamed of that. However..."

"However? There's always a however."

"However," he continued. "You seem a little... out of practice."

"A magical mess," Willow supplied. "I ruin everything."

"No you don't. I'm living proof of that. Well, *maybe* living. It sure feels like living."

"You really think it was me that made you..." she widened her eyes suggestively. "Well, you know."

"Corporal?"

She nodded conspiratorially.

"I truly do believe it was you. How else can you explain it? A century and a decade. It's almost as if I'd been waiting for you all this time. You not only have magic, Willow. You *are* magic."

She blushed. "You say that to all the ladies."

"Only witches that bring me back to life."

Willow felt a heavy awareness shift between them, and wasn't sure how she felt about it. Montgomery wasn't an ordinary guy, and even if he was, would she want to explore the possibilities between them? He might not have been a ghost anymore, but he was still moving her things around like an obsessive-compulsive poltergeist.

"Okay, here are your Cokes," Bo announced, dropping them on the table. "Do you want straws? I have to ask you that ever since the environmental committee came through here with their baseless threats."

"Straws would be great," Willow said crisply. "You know you could get paper straws to make the environmentalists happy."

"We used drinking straws made of manila in my time," said Montgomery. "There were a myriad of diseases in 1912, and straws allowed customers of the Moonstone to avoid making direct contact with the glass while drinking."

"The Moonstone." Bo said flatly. "1912."

"He's... getting into character," Willow said quickly. For the ball I'm throwing."

"You're throwing a ball?" Bo asked with raised brows.

"Yes. Next weekend. It's a costume ball and the theme is Moonstone 1912."

"The Moonstone closed in 1912," Bo said. "On

Halloween. When the owner died."

"I'm well aware," Willow said, giving Montgomery a look. "It's an *homage* to days of yore. I'll bring your invitation by tomorrow probably."

"Me? Oh no. I don't do costume parties. I don't even do Halloween except to pass out candy before the sun goes down."

"But you have to come," Willow pleaded. "There are never enough men at these things."

Bo sighed. "Will there be beer?"

"My good man," said Montgomery. "The Moonstone is known for the finest cask ales in the state."

"He's still in character," said Willow. "Yes, there will be beer."

Bo moaned. "I'll think about it. And I can't guarantee I'll be in costume if I do come, so don't get any ideas."

"Wouldn't dream of it," Willow said cheerily.

Bo grunted. "Your burgers will be right out. Just steal the ketchup from the table next to you.

"But I'm still using the ketchup," said the elderly man at the table in question.

"You're leaving soon," barked Bo, and with a harumph, turned and went into the kitchen.

"Why did he call it a costume party?" asked Montgomery.

"Because the theme is 1912, and I hate to be the one to tell you this, but what you're wearing looks like a costume."

"It certainly does not."

"Don't argue with me, grandpa. We're going shopping after this."

Montgomery scowled, and in turn, Willow blew her straw wrapper at him.

Shortly, Bo returned with the cheeseburgers, French fries, and onion rings. Montgomery was quite overcome by the aroma but as a gentleman, he waited for Willow to begin. Willow was likewise waiting for Montgomery, for she wanted to watch him take his first bite.

"After you," she said. "Prepare to be amazed."

Montgomery gathered the sandwich in both hands, eyes wide. It was a beautiful cheeseburger. A juicy char-broiled patty too big for the warm buttered bun, crispy bacon poking out, and ooey gooey cheddar cheese drip-ping down the sides. When Montgomery's mouth wrapped around the massive bun, Willow grinned, completely invested in his enjoyment of it. She was rewarded by a deep, guttural moan. She liked the sound of it, and decided she'd very much like to feed him more deli-cious things he'd never tried. Like tacos or strawberry cheesecake.

"Well?" she asked, although she knew the answer.

"It's everything I hoped for," he said.

He then tried the French fries and his whole face lit up. After devouring all of them, he declared he preferred the fries over the rings, but he'd enjoyed them both infinitely. Willow ended up splitting her burger in half and sharing it with Montgomery. He was hesitant to take it, but the thing was so big, she wouldn't have been able to finish it anyway. Besides, she liked to watch him eat. He consumed his food with such unflagging joy, she could have watched him eat all day. Smiling, she tucked the memory of it away in her heart.

When he was completely satisfied, they said goodbye to Bo and headed over to the thrift store. Willow loved thrifting. She'd found her favorite items for the bookshop in thrift stores.

"Are you ready for your glow up?" she teased Montgomery, and he responded with a hard look and eyebrow raise.

She pulled all sorts of clothing from the racks, but Montgomery was drawn to dress shirts, suspenders, and vests.

"You really are a hipster, aren't you?"

"I don't know what a hipster is," he said, "but if style and class is the defining quality, then yes."

"You sure like vests," she said, counting no less than five in his hands.

"I'm fond of waistcoats, and these are made from excellent quality wool."

"Okay, I'll tell you what. Get all the *'waistcoats'* you want. But I'm buying you some jeans."

She took him to an aisle filled with nothing but denim and Montgomery gasped.

"Dungarees," he exclaimed. "I've never owned any."

"Well, these are fifty percent off today, so take as many as you want."

But then he paused and frowned a little. "But I have no

money. I hadn't thought of that."

"It's my treat," said Willow. "Go wild."

"I cannot allow you to buy me things. It's not right."

"I just paid for our meal. What's the difference?"

"That was very generous of you, but food is a necessity and I had no choice to let you pay. I don't need clothes."

"You can't wear the same thing every day. And you'll need a toothbrush and soap and... oh geez! Underwear."

"Miss Ravensong!"

"Are you even wearing any underwear? You can't try the jeans on if you're going commando."

Montgomery lowered his voice to a whisper. "I am not without a pair of drawers... as if it's your business."

"We'll have to go to Walmart. Never buy undies at a thrift store. Do you want boxers or briefs?"

His face went completely red. "Good heavens, you're tenacious."

"I like messing with you, old man. Let's have you try this stuff on, and come out of the dressing room to show me each outfit. I want to witness your *Pretty Woman* moment."

Montgomery was either too tired or too full of bacon cheeseburger to argue, so he followed her to the dressing rooms, and tried on each item, emerging to model the clothing with several variations.

She thought he looked quite dapper, and in the end, they left with five pairs of jeans, six button downs, a couple of t-shirts, two suspenders, and all but one of the vests (or rather, waistcoats) he'd picked out.

Willow also chose a dressier outfit for him to wear to the ball, and she found the perfect gown she'd only have to modify a little bit.

As they walked back to the Moonstone with their arms full, Willow talked about all she needed to do for the ball, which meant getting the invitations out immediately.

"Will you seek out Talon Bickford today?" asked Montgomery. "Or speak to your friend Nadine about it?"

"No," Willow said thoughtfully. "Nadine said he's been rebellious lately. I think he's in with the wrong crowd or maybe he's a little cuckoo. If he really is trying to warn me about the mysterious deaths, I need to look into it more. Maybe it's just asbestos, in which case it's an easy fix."

They arrived in front of the Moonstone and Montgomery looked up at the building wearily.

"I loathe to go back in there," he said. "What if I can never leave again?"

"Do you want to walk around some more?" Willow asked. "I can take the bags inside and we could go to the park or the gazebo."

"Actually, I think I'd like to go to my grave, if that's alright with you."

Willow studied his features, noting a supernatural quality to him. His eyes glowed as if they were lit from behind. Or was that just the otherworldly proton beams?

In any case, she saw a little sadness in them.

"Are you sure?" she asked.

"Yes," he replied evenly. "I need to see it."

Willow wasn't sure where Montgomery was buried, but there was a cemetery she'd pass sometimes on her bicycle, so she decided to try that one.

"You could be anywhere in this place," she said when they arrived. "Or not even here at all. You could have been buried at sea. We should get out of here. Have you tried pizza before?"

She hated cemeteries, and was actually hoping Montgomery would change his mind.

"I'm buried here," he said solemnly. "I just know it."

He walked briskly through the iron gates and didn't slow down until he reached the older part of the graveyard —where the tombstones were worn down and cracked from age. Even though it was the middle of the day, Willow felt a bone-deep coldness creep over her as a cloud moved over the sun, and a chilly, biting wind sent crimson leaves past their heads.

Montgomery slowly wandered between the graves, checking the names. For a moment, Willow thought he'd give up soon, but then he paused in front of a large headstone, and bowed his head.

"Is it you?" Willow asked, feeling more than spooked out.

"No," he said with a melancholy chuckle. "It's Sam. He married his sweetheart from New York after all."

Willow joined Montgomery in front of the grave and read the inscription on the stone.

Sam and June Williams
Beloved parents

"There's no date," Willow said. "I wonder why."

She looked to Montgomery for an answer, but he had already moved on and stopped abruptly in front of a grave only a few plots down. The headstone was much smaller and unadorned.

Montgomery Harland
1881 - 1912

The man in front of her stood as stone still as the grave itself, and if not for the wind rustling his hair, he'd look just like a statue.

"This is more than a little creepy," she said. "Are you okay?"

He sighed. "How do I even know if my bones are in there? If I'm standing right here resurrected, then my coffin must be empty."

"Your bones are in there," Willow said. "I can feel them."

This was one of the reasons Willow hated cemeteries. Corpses resonated under her feet, like clanky windchimes.

It wasn't as if they called to her or even tremored in need of rest. She just could sense them simply existing. People and trees and inanimate objects were no different. Her body could feel anything and was always aware of the proximity of an object or person. But the bones creeped her out almost as much as a few living guys she'd met.

Montgomery didn't make her feel like that, even though logic said he should have. The truth was, Montgomery made her feel quite the opposite of creeped out.

She really knew how to pick 'em, didn't she?

He looked at her then with a peace about him Willow could only describe as some sort of closure. His eyes glittered, and the way he looked at her, she'd have considered it romantic if it weren't for the setting. For the first time, she openly admitted to herself she wanted Montgomery to kiss her. But as much as she wanted him, making out with a guy standing on his own grave was a hard pass.

She held his hand as a consolation and gazed up at him waiting for the okay to finally go home.

"What?" he said, looking at her puzzled expression. "I'm not crying again, am I?"

"No," she said with a little chuckle. "I've just never seen eyes so incredibly green before. They're like... two Midori martinis. I know that's a weird comparison."

Montgomery's face turned ashen and his brows crinkled.

"My eyes aren't green," he said, perplexed. "They're brown."

"You've always had the power,
my dear.
You just had to learn it for yourself."

—The Wizard of Oz

Chapter Fourteen

WHAT COLOR IS #THEDRESS?

"And you're telling me you see yourself with brown eyes when you look in the mirror?" Gladys, the family doctor examined Montgomery with an illumination charm shining in his face. "Hmmm. Fascinating."

"They're green, right?" Willow hollered, waving her arms at her mother and sisters. "I'm not crazy. You see it, too?"

After the trip to the cemetery, Willow decided to take Montgomery to Crescent Hollow immediately. She called Esme on the way to update her on the situation—mostly that the ghost haunting her bookshop now had a body—but also the detail about his eyes. She thought they were a wild shade of green when she first saw him as a ghost, and now she was convinced there was something else going on which she needed help figuring out.

If anyone could do it, Gladys could. Also, she was the resident expert on ghosts, having dealt with Betty Barmichael and the Miracle Whip fiasco of 1985.

"I see green," Ivy stated with authority.

"Me too," said Bliss while switching her fingernail polish back and forth between glitter and holographic.

"Thank you!" Willow cried. "I was afraid it was me. Like the thing with 'The Dress' all over again."

"It was blue and black," Ivy proclaimed.

Bliss clicked her tongue. "I saw white and gold."

"It was blue and black," said Ivy evenly. "The dress manufacturer confirmed it."

"Nevertheless," said Esme. "Everyone agrees, besides Montgomery here, that his eyes are an incandescent shade of green. Am I right?"

All the ladies, including Gladys, agreed emphatically.

"Even when we look at his reflection in the mirror at the same time," added Willow. "I see green and he sees brown. And I thought the dress was white and gold, by the way."

"What if we take a picture?" suggested Bliss.

"A photograph?" exclaimed Montgomery. "Of me? By golly."

"Tone it down, Beaver," said Willow. "You're not sitting for DaVinci, just look at Bliss's phone and smile."

"Say cheese!" Bliss sang, and snapped a picture of a wholly perplexed Montgomery. But she frowned when she checked her screen and looked up astonished. "You're not in the picture."

She turned her phone to show everyone, and there was a photo, but it only showed Gladys, who was sitting directly behind Montgomery from the camera's vantage point.

"Curiouser and curiouser," said Gladys. "You're not photographable."

"Like a vampire," said Ivy.

"He's not a vampire," Willow said. "The entire loaf of garlic bread he ate yesterday proves it."

Esme's growing concern was evidenced by the edge in her voice. "Gladys, what do you make of all this?"

"Well," said Gladys. "I've seen a lot of odd things but this one takes the cake."

"I feel *so* much better, thank you," Montgomery deadpanned.

"Do you mind if I examine you closer, dear?" Gladys asked him.

"That's why I'm here, I suppose," Montgomery replied.

Gladys wasn't an ordinary doctor. Technically, she wasn't a doctor at all. But tell that to her, and you might find your foot where your ear should be. At almost two-hundred years old, Gladys was not only respected, she was an icon. With a shock of white hair and flowing robes, her style was legendary. And although she didn't have an advanced degree, she was the best witch doctor Crescent Hollow had ever known. Even the non-magical humans called for her to administer naturopathic remedies.

But for witches (and now ghosts apparently) she didn't hold back. She reached into her carpet bag and took out a stethoscope.

"I'm going to listen to your heart, young man," she said. Then, she threw the stethoscope aside and took another tool from her bag. It was the shape of a loaf of sourdough bread with a leather string attached.

"Hold this end," she prompted, giving him the loaf of sourdough, which wasn't really a loaf of sourdough.

She held onto the end of the leather string and closed her eyes. The other women were quiet as she worked.

She nodded her head as though someone was telling her a secret. "Hmmm. Curious."

"You keep saying that. Is there cause for alarm?" Montgomery asked.

"My dear man," she said, opening her eyes. "You were a ghost two days ago and now you're sitting here having tea. We're way past alarmed."

Then she dug through her bag taking out everything but the kitchen sink and finally came up with a spyglass. She placed one end on his chest and looked through it squinting with one eye.

"I have some good news and some other news. The good news is, there is a heart in there. The other news is... it's not beating."

"Not beating?!" yelped Willow.

Gladys cleared her throat and continued. "In my professional opinion... actually I don't know. This is the weirdest case I've ever seen. But if I were to guess, I'd say this," she waved her hand up and down Montgomery's form. "is temporary. There are a few spells, but they're not really designed for this kind of thing. Mostly for crops that got frostbite or livestock that weren't doing well. The farmers had it hard; they needed a lot of magic. We don't bring people back to life. It's just not done. There are incantations and rituals for sending spirits across the veil, but there isn't any mention in any grimoire about—excuse my French—zombies."

"It's here," Bliss said. "The zombie apocalypse has begun."

"He's not a vampire and he's not a zombie," Willow said. "You guys watch too much TV."

"Zombies crawl out of their graves and drag their feet when they walk," said Ivy. "Haven't you seen the *Thriller* video?"

"They also dance," added Esme jokingly. "They're really good dancers."

"Whatever it is making your eyes glow green seems to have something to do with your case of being between worlds," Gladys said. "It is puzzling. I'll have to research the Dickens out of this one. I met him, you know. In 1842. Boston."

"Who did you meet?" Bliss asked.

"Charles Dickens, young lady. Keep up."

Willow thought it would have been the coolest thing ever to meet Charles Dickens. She wondered if she could invited Neil Gaiman to her shop for a book signing, then she could impress people in a hundred years or so.

"I would love more tea, Esme, if you please," said Galdys as if she hadn't just announced the newly corporal ghost in the living room had no heartbeat and would probably disappear at any moment. Willow was pretty much at her quota of weird crap for the day, so she accompanied Esme into the kitchen to help with the tea.

In Esme's house, there were very few things they didn't accomplish with magic. Every chore and meal were taken care of with a few choice words and a wave of the hand. But tea was a particular kind of art that Esme took very seriously. She took great care to brew the leaves in boiling water on the stovetop, straining it carefully, and transferring it into one of her many teapots. No one ever questioned her method because she was sure to emphasize that tea tastes better the slow way.

"So," said Esme, putting the water on. "Your Montgomery is quite the looker. He's no Patrick Swayze, but..."

"It's all my fault," Willow cried.

"What's your fault?"

"Montgomery seems to think it was my magic that *alived* him."

Esme hummed. "That could be."

"Then it's my fault. I messed up, just like everything else."

"Don't be so quick to blame yourself, Willow."

"Hello! He has no heartbeat."

"Did he have a heartbeat when you first met him?"

"Of course not. He was a ghost. Zephyr tried to jump into his arms once and flew right through him."

"And what exactly do you think you did to make him this way? Did you perform a chant or conjuration?"

"When he was gone those three days, I panicked a little and recited a few charms from that grimoire you sent me. But I had no idea what the heck I was doing. What if I cursed him?"

"You didn't curse him, of that I'm sure."

"Why did I even think I could try magic again? I am so bad at it. I wish I had no ability at all so at least I couldn't screw up so royally."

Esme sat down at the rustic kitchen table and urged Willow to take the next chair.

"Willow, do you think anyone with talent or abilities got it right the first time? Did Michelangelo pick up a paintbrush one day and create the masterpiece in the Sistine Chapel the next?"

"No," Willow conceded reluctantly.

"Of course not. So what makes you think, just because you have magical blood, you can perform like witches who've been at it for centuries?"

"Bliss and Ivy never blow things up or send someone's car keys into another dimension."

"Bliss and Ivy are more even tempered than you. And don't worry. Mrs. Abernathy got her keys back the same afternoon. Willow, you've always been extremely emotional. Anything you've ever tried had to be perfect the very first time, or you'd get upset and frustrated. It's a wonder you learned how to tie your own shoes."

"I do bunny ears," said Willow, looking down at her boots. Even now, she had little patience for laces and preferred slip-ons.

"You always wanted to skip the learning phase. I remember you getting so upset when you didn't get things right and that just made your magic act up even more. It was a vicious cycle. A spell would go haywire and you'd get mad at yourself, then you'd try again in a bad mood, which is never a good idea."

"Maybe I'm the one that's cursed."

"No, Pumpkin. You just need to give yourself a little grace. Discovering one's abilities is as unique as the individual herself. You've been magicking from a place of fear and over-stimulated emotions. Once you set all that aside and learn to control your feelings, I think you will be a very powerful witch. Maybe even more powerful than Bliss and Ivy put together."

The kettle whistled then, and Esme turned off the fire, pouring the water over the tea leaves. Willow loved watching her mother make tea. The flow of her arms measuring the leaves like a ballerina, the graceful way she maneuvered with the teapot as if it were an extension of her own body. Esme was Stevie Nicks, Ginger Rogers, and Lady Gaga all rolled into one incredibly beautiful and extraordinary witch. But most of all, she was the best mother Willow could ever hope for.

"Don't worry," Esme said. "I believe everything happens for a reason. And if divine destiny put Montgomery in your path, then it's all going to work out the way it's meant to be."

Esme always did know how to make someone feel better, even if they had feelings for a sort-of living ghost who might be a zombie. But actually not a zombie because zombies aren't real, and if they were real, they didn't have strong arms and kissable lips.

Willow probably had a gloomy expression on her face, and so she decided to hide behind her hands. But Esme ignored those hands and gathered her into a warm, motherly hug. Then she kissed her forehead, and peeled Willow's hands down so she could look her in the eye. As she did so, Willow's sweater sleeve slipped down her arm a little bit, exposing the shiny bracelet on her wrist.

"What's this?" asked Esme, a little curious because Willow wasn't much of a jewelry person. Too much of a hazard in her case.

"Oh it's from the Mysthaven's Women's Business Council," Willow said. "I get discounts and freebies in town with it."

Willow hadn't actually gotten any discounts or freebies yet, but she didn't get out much with so much work and a haunting to deal with.

"May I see that a little closer?" asked Esme. She turned Willow's wrist, bending and squinting to get a good look at the bracelet. "Who did you say gave this to you?"

"Um, the ladies at the Women's Council. They all had one."

This seemed to trouble Esme. "Is there an inscription?"

"I think there was a floral pattern or something. I can check if you want." Willow turned the band around her wrist, looking for the clasp, but realized the bracelet was solid all the way around. It was too snug to have fit over her hand and she couldn't remember how Jewels got it on her. There had to be a hidden clasp somewhere.

"That's funny," she puzzled. "It's like finding the end of a tape roll."

"Here, let me try," Esme offered. But she didn't have any luck either.

"Do you have any butter?" Willow was trying to squeeze the bracelet over her hand now, but her pesky thumb was in the way.

"We don't need butter," said Esme, and flicked her fingers like she always did when she wanted something done easily. But nothing happened.

Furrowing her brow, she flicked her fingers again, this time with a more dramatic woosh, and the bracelet made a ringing sound. The sound reminded Willow of a sword unsheathed from a metal scabbard.

Esme took a step back aghast. "This is a fetich. We have to get this off of you immediately."

"What just happened? Why didn't your magic work?"

"This bracelet is bound to you. Whoever put it on your wrist attached a very potent, very dark bewitchment to it. It won't come off without some extra conjuring. Thank Mother, Maid, and Crone that Gladys is here."

Esme dragged Willow by the hand out of the kitchen.

"Wait, dark bewitchment? Jewels and Daria are so nice. Nadine is kind of intense, but what do you expect from a lawyer?"

"Willow, these ladies are either extremely clueless and accidentally stumbled upon a magical object, or they're up to something wicked. I'm leaning toward the latter."

In the living room, Bliss was trying to convince Montgomery to let her cast a glamour charm on his mustache.

"You'll never have to wax it again," she said. "Imagine waking up to perfectly curled ends, not having to worry how it looks after you eat or brush your teeth... or other things you might do with your mouth."

She winked at Willow when she said the last part with a smug little look on her face. The stinker.

But Gladys seemed to know something was amiss as soon as she noticed Esme's troubled expression.

Willow showed off her bangle as Esme brought everyone up to speed, and Gladys was all over it, hovering her hand over the metal until engraved runes appeared in a purple glow.

सन्ध्यापर्दः कन्याः

"I know this," said Gladys with a look of horror. "Every witch I've seen wearing one of these circlets is as vile as they are beautiful. And they are all beautiful, believe me... using black arts to maintain their vanity and unnatural long life. Longer even than any other witch or wizard."

That did sound about right as far as Willow could tell. Come to think of it, the ladies at Nadine's house had abnormally contrived good looks, but she just thought it was the result of a lot of makeup or Botox.

"They're known as a powerful and wicked coven and were banished from Salem even before the witch trials. Even Crescent Hollow washed their hands of them. They call themselves the Daughters of the Twilight Veil."

"Talon Bickford," Montgomery blurted. "He was trying to warn you about something."

"Or he's up to no good," Willow countered. "Doing his mother's dirty work. Whatever that is."

"But what do they want with you?" Ivy wondered.

"Trying to get her to join their coven," Bliss suggested. Why else would they slap that thing on her wrist?"

"Why would there be witches in Mysthaven?" Willow questioned. "There's no community there."

"It does sit on the same ley line as Crescent Hollow," said Esme.

"What is a ley line?" Montgomery asked.

"They're paths along land and sky," replied Esme. "Kind of like magical rivers."

"Or, in scientific terms," added Willow. "Electromagnetic channels of Earth's energy. Stonehenge sits on a ley line."

"And we're on one now?" Montgomery asked.

"They're all over the world," Willow said. "It's really no big deal."

"I seem to recall you had a relative involved with that coven," said Gladys to Esme. "Was it a cousin or an aunt?"

Esme racked her memory. "Maybe my great aunt Celeste? I've never met her but I heard she was a little out there. Nobody knows what happened to her. She just disappeared one day."

"Is there someone named Celeste in your women's group?" Ivy asked. "Perhaps she wanted a family connection or something."

Willow shook her head vaguely. "No. Not unless they weren't using their real names."

"I think I have a picture of her," Esme said, moving to the armoire. "There's a photo album in here somewhere."

She found a book full of photos in a drawer of the armoire after a minute, then sat down with Willow on the sofa to go through it. Everyone, including Montgomery, crowded around them to see.

Esme gingerly turned the aged pages of the book poring through a century and a half of family photos. About a third of the way, she came across a sepia-colored image of a woman from about the turn of the twentieth century. Her face had a doll-like quality, with round cheeks, large eyes, and a small, heart-shaped mouth. Slim waisted (probably the effect of an organ crushing corset), in a long-sleeved bustle dress, she posed with a parasol in her hand, and beneath a smart wide-brimmed hat, was a puff of blonde curls and ringlets. She was simply stunning, and something told Willow she was an artless, natural beauty. So why on earth would she care to associate herself with the Daughters of the Twilight Veil?

"I don't recognize her," said Willow.

But what astonished her the most were the words that next fell from Montgomery's lips.

"I do," he said gravely. "She's the woman with the golden curls."

"THE UNDISCOVERE'D COUNTRY,
FROM WHOSE BOURN
NO TRAVELLER RETURNS."

-William Shakespeare

Chapter Fifteen

BEING ALIVE

Funny how selective memory works. Montgomery didn't remember much about Celeste Ravensong except that hers was the last face he saw before he died. And she was crying.

For the next day or two, he turned it over and over in his head, clawing into the stores of his memory. He knew she'd come to the Moonstone Saloon all alone, and would return frequently, often staying for hours. He was always so busy, though. Her face sped by so fast in his thoughts, it was almost in a blur of feathers and golden curls.

But then something stuck. She wore a gold chain which she'd absently clutch to her chest as if it brought her comfort. From it dangled an emerald gem, and would swing from her neck like a pendulum. And then, Montgomery had the sinking sense that this woman loved him, even though he could not love her back.

When he told this to Willow, she cringed a little, and tried to urge him to remember more. Was he completely certain he didn't love her great great aunt Celeste? Did they have an understanding? Had he led her on?

Montgomery knew in his heart there was only one answer to those questions: no.

In the week that followed, they developed a rhythm of existing in the same space physically. Montgomery slept on the floor of Willow's office, would rise with the sun, make coffee before Dale arrived for work, and proved himself useful behind the bar. Willow had to assure Dale that she would not cut his hours, since her 'boyfriend' wasn't on the payroll.

Willow considered canceling the ball, but Montgomery convinced her it was best not to let on that she knew the Women's Business Council was just a front for a wicked coven.

Also, it would be a good opportunity to observe the

Daughters of the Twilight Veil surreptitiously, and figure out what kind of bad hocus pocus they were up to.

When the night finally arrived, and guests were on their way, Montgomery waited downstairs for Willow in the transformed bookshop. Shelves were covered in thick, velvet drapery that matched the cushions on the barstools, and the only source of lighting was the chandelier and a few sconces.

He cast around, checking on all the details. Trays of finger foods, a signature drink for the evening, and all the bar garnishes were in place. And as he turned toward the footsteps announcing Willow's arrival from her upstairs rooms, Montgomery's heart skipped a beat. Or it would have if it was actually beating.

She wore a white gown encrusted with shimmering beads and dramatic sleeves spilling off her exposed shoulders. Her hair was piled high upon her head and a soft waterfall of curls spilled from the crown where a single white ostrich feather sat, ornamented with a bejeweled brooch.

He was stunned into a stupor from her beauty.

She smiled as she approached him, raking her eyes up and down his form.

"You clean up well," she said impishly then added, "For a robot."

She'd taken to calling him a robot lately, (whatever that was) in place of the alternative, which was either zombie, vampire, living dead, or animated corpse. None of which accurately described his plight, by the way. He decided to just go with it. He couldn't do anything about it anyway. And whatever was happening to him was infinitely preferable to floating around as a ghost.

"Did you see to it there is to be no photography?"

"Check," she said brightly. "All phones and modern devices will be checked at the door. No one's allowed to bring anything in that didn't exist in 1912."

The plan was for Montgomery to work the bar and be essentially invisible to the guests who hardly notice the staff at these things. If he was lucky, he would overhear odds and ends of conversations or meaningful glances between the ladies of the coven, and hopefully piece together their purpose for Willow.

Guests arrived in couples and groups, townspeople he'd seen in the bookshop over the past few weeks. The construction worker named Kyle came in a wool suit accompanied by a woman that was most likely his wife. He introduced the woman to Willow who smiled amiably, then the couple moved on to the appetizers.

Bo arrived in what barely counted as accurate clothing from 1912, but he at least wore a flat cap. Of course, no man would be caught dead in a flat cap at an upscale social gathering, but when it came to dead, who was Montgomery to judge?

He watched as guests mingled and ordered drinks, and thought for a time that the coven sisters weren't coming. But an hour into the festivities, they came through the door illuminated from behind by the moonlight, turning every male head in the building. He stepped into the darkness to remain hidden from them, but he didn't recognize any of the ladies from his time, and then decided it was safe they wouldn't recognize him either. How awkward would that have been?

The four of them split up almost immediately upon arrival, drifting to each corner of the shop as if they were winds of the North, South, East, and West. They had an otherworldly way about them, and Montgomery wondered how Willow could not recognize other witches when she saw them. He could tell there was something off about them right away. But maybe he was predisposed to see them in that light.

After a time, one of the ladies drifted over to the bar and ordered a gin martini. She had dark hair, high cheekbones, and an extremely fierce look about her. He surmised she was the one Willow described as Nadine Bickford, but couldn't be sure. All the women that came in with her seemed pretty intense.

Then she did something he hadn't expected. She gazed at him for an uncomfortable length of time, tilting her head ever so slightly.

"I've not seen you before," she said in a silken voice. "And I know everyone in Mysthaven, even if they don't know me."

She chuckled daintily and looked him over. "What's your name?"

Montgomery held her gaze for a long moment, all hopes of anonymity dashed. But he wouldn't lose his cool. "It's quite a feat," he said coolly. "To know every person."

"I make it my business," she replied, matching his tone. "As a lawyer."

Ah, so she was Nadine. Willow mentioned she owned a law firm, but the other partners didn't seem to exist.

"Well, I've only been here for a spell," he said. "You could say I'm new."

"Hmmm. Then welcome to Mysthaven. And if you need any legal advice, ask around for Nadine."

"And if you need another martini, you can ask around for Mountie."

Just then, Montgomery caught Willow's eye, and as Nadine slinked into the crowd, he gave a reassuring nod to indicate it was okay.

All through the night Willow was the consummate hostess, encouraging her guests to dance and eat the seemingly endless trays of bite-sized food.

What amused Montgomery the most was seeing Dale dressed to the nines in an historically accurate tuxedo, dancing the waltz with a young woman he assumed was his new girlfriend. The couple took to the dance floor with the ease of seasoned dancers, and flowed into perfectly timed steps—Dale with his carriage straight, and arms squarely boxed.

"I wonder if there is a gentleman present who will ask me to dance," said Willow, having come up alongside him during a lull in cocktail orders.

"I believe there is a certain gentleman who would

want nothing more than to dance with you," Montgomery replied. "If he could afford the distraction."

"Our four women of interest are mingling by the dance floor. We'd have a better chance of eavesdropping over there."

"Somehow I doubt they'd openly discuss their evil plans in a crowded room."

"This party is their chance to roam around my book-shop and leave little hexes all over or snoop around the place. If they try anything, I'll be able to sense the magic pouring out of them before they can say abracadabra. Besides, Esme cast a rebounding charm on all the drapery. Whatever magic they try to do in here will bounce right back to them."

"Ah. So the drapery isn't just for the aesthetic."

"That too." She smiled up at him, and in that moment, he couldn't be bothered with drapery or witches or being half-dead. He only wanted to take this beautiful woman in his arms.

"In that case," he said with a slight bow. "May I have this dance, Miss Ravensong?"

"You may, Mr. Harland."

He offered to take her hand, and when she slipped her fingers into his waiting palm, a current bolted through his body.

He'd only danced a handful of times, and even so, one would think he'd be rusty after such a long time. But Willow put him at ease, and as he slid his arm around her back, he felt a lightness envelop them, and they fell into the steps easily.

"I've been wanting to say," Willow said softly as they grew closer to one another, "thank you for washing my dishes. And mopping the floor. And cleaning up the Bloody Mary mix that one night."

"You don't need to thank me for doing something I did on my own accord. I hadn't thought how it would scare you. I was selfish and wasn't used to sharing the space with someone."

"I want you to know I'm not a complete slob. I was overtired that week. And truth be told, the way I was brought up, Esme taught us to clean up our messes with a swoosh of the wrist. Except I would usually make a bigger mess. So Bliss and Ivy did all the housework. That's one of the reasons why I left home. I wanted to prove I could do something without help."

"People need people," said Montgomery. "Being alone isn't as fun as I make it seem."

"I promise to be a better roommate from now on," she continued. "No more messes, and I'll get better at doing th—"

He shushed her by gently pressing his lips over hers. It was just a touch, and lasted a half a second at that. But it was the most glorious sensation Montgomery had ever felt. He felt it by the tingle in his lips to the prickling on his skin, down to his toes.

"I don't want to talk about housework, Miss Ravensong. I'm trying to dance with the most beautiful woman in the room."

She blinked up at him with a dazed expression. "Maybe I should keep talking so you can shut me up like that again."

"Keep talking, and I fear I might throw you over my shoulder and shut you up another way."

Her face lit up like the flame of a candle. "Why Mister Harland. You sure know how to woo a lady."

He was about to respond by telling her that as a gentleman, he didn't do things in halves (except staying dead, apparently), and if he'd gone that route, he'd have blabbed something truly regretful, like saying he'd only partake in carnal knowledge with a woman if joined in nuptial union. Willow was a woman of the twenty-first century. Surely, he thought, she'd dismiss his values as outdated and archaic. Still, that is where he stood.

But he had no such opportunity to embarrass himself in such a tender and lovely moment. The tender and lovely moment was soiled by the movement he caught in the corner of his eye.

Nadine was near the back of the shop, signaling to her coven sisters to follow her into the rear hallway. Now, if it were any other women, he would have assumed they were going to the bathroom, as women love to go together. But there were more than bathrooms in the back hallways of the shop. There was the kitchen, the dry food storage, the supply room, and Willow's office. The office where they had all the evidence of their investigation of the mysterious deaths of all the owners of the building. Including his own.

In an effort to not raise suspicion he was looking their way, he clutched Willow to his chest and whispered in her ear. "Don't look now, but the Twilight ladies are headed to your office."

"There's a light enchantment over the doorway," Willow whispered back. "They can't get in."

"Do you want to risk it?" he warned. "Gladys said their ways are dark and powerful. Don't you think they can get through your wall of sparkles and glitter?"

"I only added the glitter for fun," she said. "The sparkles are part of the spell."

As he held Willow against him, Montgomery looked over her shoulder just as the four Daughters of the Twilight Veil disappeared through the hallway entryway.

"We should stop them," he said against her neck, and part of him wanted to stay on the dance floor and just forget about everything else. Wicked witches who? But he knew they had to do something even if their efforts were futile.

"And say what when we run into them?" Willow whispered.

"It's your office," he reminded her. "They're the ones sneaking around.

"Oh. Yeah. Right."

Montgomery led Willow by the hand off the dance floor and into the back hallways, but the coven was nowhere to be found. They looked in the office, the kitchen, the store room. All the places.

"Maybe they did just go to the bathroom," he said, puzzled. "Do you think they left out the back door?"

"Well that would be completely rude not to say good-bye," she replied.

They decided to go back into the office, and closing the door behind them, made sure all the documents and research notes were locked away somewhere no one would think to look. Inside a locked and enchanted titanium box, inside a locked and enchanted chromium box, inside an enchanted Costco-sized box of feminine napkins, sealed with packing tape.

"Everything's in order," said Willow. "No one's tampered with the box or the many enchantments."

Montgomery rather liked being in the office with Willow alone, dressed in their finery, with a little wine running through their veins. In fact, he would have loved to remain there with her until all the guests went home, meanwhile tasting those delectable lips again. Yes, he was one-minded. But could anyone blame the man after the longest dry spell in history?

Then again, he was very much a gentleman, and he felt it necessary to discuss his intentions, however bad the timing.

"Willow," he began, "about the—"

Upon hearing footsteps, he fell silent. There seemed to be four sets of feet. He hoped it was all his imagination.

But it wasn't.

A moment later, there came a jiggling of the doorknob, and although he and Willow had every right to be there, he panicked and swiftly pulled Willow with him into the smallest coat closet imaginable. He closed the closet door with a soft click right before the outer door opened force-fully, and women's voices could be heard spilling inside.

At first, all he could hear were mumblings and little complaints in hushed tones. His back was pressed all the way to the back of the closet and the only light came from beneath the door jam. He could only make out Willow's darkened silhouette, and from the close proximity to her, could smell nothing but her soft, floral perfume and the natural scent of her skin. It was now his favorite scent in the world.

Her body had nowhere to go but to lean against him. Her body a breath away from his, her lips excruciatingly close. He ached to have her, and even as his arms held her into his chest, he fought to exercise restraint.

Next, he heard one voice say, "Are we ready sisters?"

Then another voice replied, "It is close. Soon we will be complete."

Complete? What did they mean by that? Was Willow joining the coven what would make them complete? Something about the number five? He could only guess.

"How do you find the charge, Astrid?" another witch said. She sounded like Nadine.

He recognized the voice of Astrid from when she dealt with the building's real estate transfer.

"The charge is as it should be, almost ripe for the pick-ing," Astrid replied. "I sense it calling for us."

These women were as cryptic as could be. If he'd overheard any other group of women talking like this, he'd think they'd been drinking too much. At this point, he wouldn't be surprised if they started chanting *'Double, double, toil and trouble.'*

"Good," said Nadine. "We will stay and act merry for another short while. Then we will take our leave and rest. There is much to do."

Montgomery felt Willow shift under him, her shoulders quaking in his embrace. He squeezed her into him, and felt her head pivot up. And then her lips were so close, he could feel the barely-there tickle of their touch. The smallest movement, and her mouth would be on his. And this time, he wouldn't hold back.

The ladies of the coven lingered inside the office for another minute, one of them lamenting her choice of shoes. When they closed the door behind them and the office fell silent, he didn't let go of Willow. He did the opposite of let go. His hands drifted up her shoulders, tracking their way up her neck, and landing on her face, gently cupping her cheeks.

"I didn't ask permission to kiss you before," he said. "And so I'm asking you now—"

"Yes!" she blurted. "And if you ask me again, I'll clobber you."

He lowered his head then and took her mouth with the fervor and ardor of a first and last kiss all rolled into one. She seemed to meld into him, their lips so warm, there was no telling where one ended and the other began.

She giggled. "Your mustache tickles."

"You like it," he moaned into her mouth, kissing her deeper until she sagged into him, nails sinking into his sides.

Greedily, he pulled her closer until there was no more space between them, his chest tightening as he kissed her with every ounce of passion he could stand. Her gasps sent a shiver through him, and he felt buoyant and so alive.

Alive.

"I'm afraid I'm addicted to you, Miss Ravensong," he rasped into the kiss. "We'll have to live in this closet from now on."

She clung to him. "As long as someone brings us food, I'm okay with that."

Gliding his fingertips gently down her neck and shoulders, chest aching to devour her, he said brokenly, "We should go back to the party."

"Yeah," she said absently. "Sure."

Even as she whispered the words, her teeth scraped over his bottom lip and all reason went out the window.

He met her in the kiss stroke for stroke, surrounding her with his arms, giving her his whole soul, consuming all he could, and yet, with a measure of careful tenderness.

Breathing hard, he pressed his forehead to hers, taking her face in his hands. "If we don't stop right now..."

"I know," she said, panting a little. "People will wonder where we are."

"And I think Dale was making drinks last time I checked."

"Oh no. That could turn into a disaster."

He stroked a strand of her hair back into place. "How about you take a minute to freshen up while I make you a cocktail?"

"That sounds perfect," she said. "Surprise me?"

"I'll come up with something."

With a quick kiss, he opened the closet door, smiling bashfully in the warm light of the office, and went back to the party.

He was just in time to see the coven take their leave out the front door. Relieved, he headed to the bar where Dale was flipping shakers and glassware behind his back.

After a round of applause from the few people gathered around him, he took a small bow.

"I've watched *Cocktail* on DVD hundreds of times, studying the moves," he bragged.

Montgomery crossed his arms, giving Dale a hard stare. "Should I leave you to it, friend?"

Dale swept a bar towel over his shoulder and yawned. "I think I'll call it a night."

He swaggered out from behind the bar and joined his female friend who was grinning at him proudly. Apparently Dale's bartending skills impressed her.

The crowd was dwindling at this point, and Willow emerged from the office looking perfectly put together. Montgomery felt so light, he wondered if he might float through the ceiling.

He'd mixed her a cocktail with Irish whiskey, sour apple schnapps and cranberry juice, shook vigorously, straining it into a chilled martini glass lined with caramel drizzle, then garnished it with an apple slice.

"I thought this might appeal to you," he said to Willow when she reached the bar. He slid it to her, and poured himself two fingers of single malt scotch.

Willow grinned brilliantly. "The color of your eyes."

"I wanted to do something besides Midori," he said. "Something reminiscent of those cookies you make."

"Caramel apple crunchies?"

"The ones with cranberries."

"Oh, the cran-apple delights?"

"Whatever you call them, they're delicious."

He brought the glass to his lips, almost too happy and grinny to take a sip. He looked into her shining eyes, the way they glimmered with a secret. That kiss.

She winked, bringing the green cocktail to her lips. And a flash of déjà vu jolted him, like the skipping of a record he'd heard all those years ago when the Moonstone sold those vinyl disks.

But it wasn't just sound that skipped just now. It was a vision, and suddenly he was there behind the bar, taking a sip as a woman with shining, glimmering eyes ran to him from across the crowded bar.

"Don't drink that," he cried, slapping the martini glass out of Willow's hand just before it touched her lips. The glass flew across the bar, splashing the green liquid onto the floor, the glass breaking just beyond the puddle.

Willow yelped, and looked down upon her white

dress, now splattered with green drops of liquor. Her gaze lifted to Montgomery, horrified, alarmed, confused.

"Why did you just do that?" she wailed.

To which Montgomery answered gravely, "I know how I died."

"EVERY DAY IS HALLOWEEN, ISN'T IT?
FOR SOME OF US."

—Tim Burton

Chapter Sixteen

TICKLE ME EMO

I t was Monday. Two days until Halloween. About three twenty-six in the afternoon.

Currently, Willow was hiding away all the apple schnapps, just in case. She wasn't ready to throw it out. She'd paid good money for it, after all. So, she figured a locked cabinet was an adequate transition spot. Sort of like when you're not ready to put your clothes in the hamper so you drape them over a chair.

Montgomery tried to reason with her.

"For the last time, *your* martini wasn't poisoned. It was a knee jerk reaction once the memory flashed before me."

"Whatever you say, Snow White."

She had taken to calling him Snow White almost immediately after he told her he died by poison. Of course, he didn't understand any of her modern pop culture references, so why should this one be any different? He usually nodded vaguely, which Willow found more amusing than anything. He also was quick to point out that although the poisoned liquor he drank that night in 1912 was green, it certainly wasn't apple schnapps. Someone must have slipped something in his scotch without him knowing. It wasn't until he'd already sipped it did he notice the color. A bright, bioluminescent green.

Still, death by poisoned apple schnapps? How often can you say that happens? And to be able to tease the deceased about it? Priceless.

Not to make fun of murder, by any means. But really, it had been over a century. Whoever killed Montgomery was long gone by now.

So, she'd called him Snow White the rest of the evening, and throughout the next day, dropping the fairy tale books in front of him and playing *Someday My Prince Will Come* and *Whistle While You Work* over the shop's speakers on repeat.

Dale enjoyed the latter, and whistled along, much to Montgomery's chagrin.

"I wonder if that's why your eyes turned green," she said, turning it over in her mind.

"I don't think that's how poison works," he said. "Then again, nothing really makes sense anymore. I shouldn't even be breathing, but here I am."

"Here you are," Willow marveled, then walked over toward the cash register to close it out. It had been a remarkably slow day for sales, and Dale had somewhere he wanted to be, so they closed early.

But as she went, she found her eye drawn to the corner of the room where that blasted purple velvet box sat on a low shelf.

"Very funny, Tin Man," she said, stomping over and snatching it off the shelf. "I don't want this on display. Stop moving it."

Montgomery answered her with mild bewilderment. "I didn't move that."

"Nice try, but I know it was you," she said with some measure of irritation. "You've been pranking me for weeks. I'm hiding the key this time."

She locked it up once again in a cabinet and slipped the key in that little pocket in her jeans that has no other use other than to store a single key or maybe a coin. She told herself she'd better remember it was there before doing laundry.

"I truly do not know what you're talking about," said Montgomery. "I haven't touched your box."

"It's not mine," she explained. "It belongs to the—"

She gasped, cutting herself off with a lightbulb thought. Then she turned with wide eyes and slack jaw to an equally wide-eyed and slack jawed Montgomery. He must be putting it all together before she could say the words.

"Daughters of the Twilight Veil," they both said in concert. Over the past week, they'd been calling the coven the *'Twihards'* to be economical in word use, (and because Willow loved a good book to movie fandom nickname) but this moment called for the full title.

(By the way, she was Team Edward).

"You have to get rid of it," Montgomery said urgently. "Throw it outside in the big trash bin. Or toss it in a lake."

"If you haven't been moving it, and Dale hasn't been moving it, yet it keeps moving, then it's safe to say it moves on its own."

"It will find its way back here?" Montgomery cried. "That's rather spooky."

"Dude! You are a literal ghost who came back to life and is walking around without a beating heart. What exactly are you gauging your spooky meter on?"

"What is in that box, Willow?"

"A crystal ball. Astrid told me she bought it at Hobby Lobby. I get it now that she was lying."

Willow laughed, remembering something.

"What's so funny?"

"Astrid made a joke when she handed it to me. Like she was pretending it was some ancient relic. The Orb of

Gorimaan or something. She wasn't serious about that was she?"

"It would be a roundabout way of telling you what it really is without you believing it."

"Maybe it's some Twihard rule that you have to say what it is when you pass it along," Willow wondered.

"What are you going to do with it then?"

She sighed, looking at the cabinet door as if the thing inside was mocking her.

"I don't know. Astrid gave it to me to use as a prop for my fortune telling booth at the harvest festival. I guess I was supposed to give it back to her when I was done with it."

Montgomery eyed the cabinet in the same way Willow did. "Hmmm. They obviously have something planned for it."

"Maybe it's set up to seep out dark magic all over the crowd and they needed someone—AKA me—to do their dirty work," Willow said. It was as plausible an explanation as any.

They both stood there, staring at the cabinet in silence as if they were waiting for it to unlock on its own for the purple velvet box to come flying out. But it's like waiting for a pot of water to boil. Nothing ever happens when you're looking.

After a long while, they went back to the lounge area and sat down, and Montgomery said softly,

"I am sorry about your gown."

"Nothing a little magic won't fix," Willow replied with

a chuckle. "As long as I don't accidentally turn the whole dress green. And how do we know the Twihards *didn't* tamper with the booze? While we were... ehem. You know. Otherwise engaged."

He blushed a little at that which must have been a very difficult thing to do with nothing to pump the blood through his veins.

"It was a lovely thing," he said stoically. "I want you to know I'd never felt such joy in life or after. And if some-thing were to happen to me..."

"Nothing's going to happen to you."

Montgomery sighed, standing from his seat, and pulled her up into his arms, kissing the crown of her head. She'd never felt more safe. Imagine. A man half living would be the one to protect her.

"Willow," he continued, cupping her face to look her in the eyes. "Whatever it is I'm made of, it's not meant to last. You know this."

"No, I don't. Gladys could be a complete quack. We should get a second opinion."

"I can feel it," he countered. "Can we just make the most of the time we do have?"

He kissed her then, soft, warm lips caressing hers. Confident hands curling around her back, making her pulse fly. And she had a distant thought—how could he be so warm? His body, his skin, his breath... well, it all felt very much like touching a living man. An elegant, solid man with a little scruff on his jaw. The scruff wasn't there last night.

She was just luxuriating in the kiss when a jingle came from the front door, announcing a customer had entered the shop.

She hazily let it register that she'd forgotten to lock it for the night and blinked when Montgomery pulled away, giving her a quick peck on the lips before jerking his head in the direction of the door.

Loath to tear herself away from him, she walked toward the front of the shop to inform the customer they were closed and to please leave so she could continue making out with her recently alive boyfriend. That last part she'd keep to herself.

But then, she stopped dead in her tracks when she saw who'd just entered.

Talon Bickford.

Still in the same emo uniform, she mused, noting the black clothes, black coat, black expression. It was those sunken cheeks that did it for her. If he wasn't such a sinister creature, he'd arouse a tortured, Edward Scissorhands sort of compassion for anyone who saw the sallow look in his eyes.

Willow crossed her arms and gave him a hard look. He didn't scare her one bit or invoke compassion for that matter.

But Montgomery, having only second-hand knowledge, and a building ire toward the man for startling Willow, was not so passive in his greeting.

He charged toward him, fists at his sides, growling like a bear. Never mind that Talon was likely a wielder of dark magic and could take anyone out, let alone a hundred-and forty-year-old tin man without a heart.

"Why are you here, and you better make it quick," Montgomery snarled.

Talon tossed a dismissive glance at Montgomery before sliding his eyes onto Willow.

"I warned you, didn't I? And yet you don't heed my words."

"Can you be any less cryptic?" Willow snapped. "We're not living in a Tim Burton movie."

"I told you to stay away."

"Stay away from what, exactly?" She half-laughed. "The water? Too many carbs? Screen time?"

"The Daughters of the Twilight Veil came here last night invited. You must never invite dark forces into your edifice. You don't know what they're capable of."

"You know, this would have been great information to have if I had met you before. Oh wait. We did meet. When you were too busy channeling Vincent Price to give me details."

"Is that all you came to say?" Montgomery snarled. "Because we already know your mother is bad news."

Talon snickered. "Where did you find this guy? Did he come with the building?"

"Something like that," Willow said. "Now please get on with whatever you have to say or leave."

Talon jerked his chin. "You're still wearing the Circlet of Nebula."

Willow glanced at the bracelet around her wrist. "Is that what it's called? It won't come off."

"It will come off," he replied. "But it takes a certain kind of magic. Do you know why they bound it on you?"

"I have a few theories."

"They need you in their coven. There's something they want in this building, and you're the one with the keys."

"Why didn't they just buy it themselves? Astrid literally handed me the keys."

"There's a centuries old curse on the coven," Talon said. "They can neither buy nor sell land or any structure upon it. It was meant to make them wander, never to settle anywhere."

"And why should we listen to you?" Montgomery questioned. "You're one of them."

"No, I'm not." Talon seemed truly offended for the first time. "I hate my mother. I hate everything she stands for."

"And that's why you refused to work here in the shop when she asked you?" Willow guessed.

"They never told me what they wanted me to do for them here. I didn't want to set foot in this shop."

"Yet here you are," said Montgomery. "In the shop."

"You could have been just like them," he said to Willow. "How could I have known until now?"

"What's changed now?"

"There's a different kind of magic about you. It took me a while to sense it. You're not like my mother."

"I still don't understand what they want from me."

"The Daughters of the Twilight Veil, as I mentioned before, wandered everywhere after being cast out of Salem. This was almost four hundred years ago, so naturally, over the centuries some of them abandoned the coven in search of something else. That didn't bode well with the other witches. There's a rumor the ones who left met a treacherous end. I'm not sure of the details. All I know, is the remaining members came up with a bond to devote their lives to the coven forever, and that's when the Circlet of Nebula came about."

Willow clutched the bracelet around her wrist, thinking of the terrible noise it made when Esme tried her magic on it.

"My mother never was good at communication," Talon continued. "She wouldn't tell me what she's up to if I begged. My guess is there's something she wants and owning this building—either through inheritance or family connection—is the only way to get it. And since you're part of her sisterhood now, it's as good as hers."

Willow didn't like the sound of all this. But it still didn't all add up. How could a silly bracelet make her one of them? Dear lord, she was a Twihard!

"What about the house she lives in? She doesn't own it?"

Something about the idea of a powerful witch having to pay rent to a landlord cracked her up. She'd get evicted if her witchery was ever found out.

"She inherited it from her third husband in 1883. He'd built it for her, apparently."

"Your mom's *that* old? How old are you?"

"I'm twenty-one. And before you ask, I don't know my father. He died when I was a baby. I'm not saying she hexed him, but I'm not saying she didn't, either. He just died unexpectedly."

"Sounds like a common trend with this town," Montgomery said.

"Talon, I need you to answer me honestly. Do you think your mother had anything to do with the deaths of the owners of this building?"

"I really couldn't say for sure. Only one."

A lump formed in the pit of her stomach. "Which one?"

"There was a witch who was lured into the coven at a young age. She was impressionable and stupid, according to my mother. But she was extremely beautiful and had a talent for making any man fall for her. Superficially, of course. So, they charged her to get the original owner of the Moonstone to marry her, so she'd inherit it for the coven. They had some kind of plan, I'm not sure what. But it all went sideways when the young witch fell madly in love with the man. His name was... Mortimer or Montgomery or something. And when he refused her, she went a little crazy and poisoned him."

Willow gasped. "Celeste."

"Yeah. I think that's her name. Anyway, after that, the building changed hands over a dozen times. Only a few businesses actually made it to the opening stage. Something would always happen, and it usually didn't end well for the property owners."

He sliced his thumb across his neck to emphasize his point.

Montgomery was stone silent and had to brace himself on the counter.

"I feel like I'm going to be sick," Willow said.

"They'll stop at nothing," warned Talon. "But none of the previous owners of this property have been a witch. You're the first one. And whatever it is that interests them in this place, they'll try to get it through you."

"Whatever happened to Celeste?" Willow asked.

Talon shrugged. "Maybe she's dead. Or got turned into a lamppost. Nobody knows."

"I certainly hope it's neither," Willow said. "Maybe she flew away on her broomstick and is sipping piña coladas on a tropical beach somewhere."

Talon gave her a flat look. He seemed like he'd probably burn to a crisp on a tropical beach without a 5000 SPF sunblock. And he didn't strike her as a piña colada guy either. He was more of a *getting stuck in the rain* type.

"I brought you this," he said after an uncomfortable moment, and produced a worn, leatherbound book from inside his coat. "I stole it from my mother. It's full of the blackest spells, brews, and incantations ever written. I would not dare to use it under any other circumstances. But if it helps you against my mother and those other old hags, it might be your best bet."

Willow took the book with some trepidation. What could possibly go wrong with a book of dark curses and an ancient drabardi crystal ball in her possession?

Talon left after he handed over the book. He didn't say goodbye or see ya later or anything pleasant like that. He just turned around and left.

"Wow, he sure monologued for a long time for a guy who couldn't be bothered to talk a couple weeks ago," Willow said after the door shut behind him. She immediately locked it.

"Such an odd man," Montgomery said.

"Considering his upbringing, I'd say he could be much weirder than that."

Montgomery tipped his chin toward the book in Willow's hands. "You're not going to use that, are you?"

"No. Of course not," she said defensively. "But it might give me some clues about why Nadine wants the Moonstone so badly and what she plans to do with it."

She shook a little, trembling as she held the book, and Montgomery placed a warm palm over her hands, then gently took the book from her, placing it on the counter.

"Now I know why you could see me from the first day you came here. How I was brought back into a corporal form. You were always meant to help me. A descendant of the woman who murdered me and it's all coming full circle. If anyone can stand up against Nadine, it's you. It's always been you."

"I feel like I'm terribly underqualified for the *'Chosen One'* role," she said dismissively.

"So was Frodo Baggins. But isn't that what makes the victory all so much more remarkable?"

A small smile cracked at the corner of Willow's mouth. Montgomery and his Hobbit books.

"We could leave," she said. "Go to New Zealand and live in a warm, cozy hole in the ground."

"No," he said gently, and gave her a soft kiss. "You're going to be the hero I know you were meant to be."

His thumb traced the line of her jaw. Bowing down, he curled his finger under her chin and tilted her head up to him, closing his lips around hers. Tasting her, consuming her.

She clung to him, digging her fingers into his shirt, wrenching him closer until she had the feeling his body was both crushing into her, and not close enough.

"Remind me to call you a hero more often if this is the reward I get," he said breathlessly, tangling his fingers in her hair. He wrapped a strand of curls around his hand and pulled gently to coax her head back. The feel of his mustache along the column of her neck and the growth of scruff on his jaw sent all the wooshy sensations to her belly.

"Do you think you can... uh... I don't know... are you..." Willow could hardly think straight let alone speak in full sentences.

"Are you asking me if... everything's in working order?" he asked.

She felt a rush of heat fill her cheeks and immediately regretted bringing it up. She had to remember she was making out with a ghost. A ghost! Or something like a ghost. They still hadn't figured out exactly what he was.

"I... think we should get some dinner. Being close to you is making me forget myself."

"You need never be ashamed or embarrassed with me," he said tenderly. "That being said, I could do with a nice meal."

"Should we order in or eat out?"

"Definitely eat out," he replied with a smile so sparkly and beautiful, Willow felt her heart crack a little.

"Okay, let me just grab my purse and we'll figure out where we want to go."

Montgomery waited by the front of the shop while she ran upstairs to get her coat and purse. She rushed to get back, only having been gone for a minute. But when she returned, he was on the floor.

"Monty!" She flew to him and knelt down in a panic. "Monty! You better stay with me, or I swear I'll—"

"You'll what?" he mumbled. His eyes opened in slits, and he looked like... well, he looked like exactly what he was. Death warmed over. Groggily, he turned his head to face her hovering over him.

"What happened?" he said wearily.

"I think you collapsed," she said, her voice still shaky with worry. "Are you okay? I'll call Gladys."

"Don't call Gladys. I just blacked out for a minute, that's all."

"Was it a stroke? Blood pressure? Imbalance of the humors?"

Montgomery tried to smile, but he seemed too weak. Willow ran to the bar, wetting a towel, and returned to fold it over his forehead. This gave him some reprieve, and after a short while, he tried to get up, but couldn't do so without her help.

He leaned on Willow's shoulder as she walked him to the office where he had a cot for sleeping.

"I hate this for you," she said. "Can you make it upstairs to rest in my bed?"

"I would," he replied cheekily, "but how do I know you won't take advantage of me?"

"I might, but not until you feel better."

At least he felt well enough to joke. As soon as she got him tucked in, she was going to call Esme and Gladys despite his wishes to the contrary.

He hobbled into the office, insisting the cot was more than adequate, and waited on the desk chair while Willow made up his bedding.

"Your kiss," he said as his head hit the pillow. "excited my delicate nature. I dare say, Miss Ravensong, you have made me swoon."

"Next time I'll bring my smelling salts," she replied. "Now try to rest. I'll order some chicken soup from Bo's."

She swept a lock of his hair from his forehead and kissed him gingerly. And after he had eaten and fallen asleep, she wept with debilitating worry.

"iT'S AS MUCH FUN To SCARE
AS To BE SCARED."

-Vincent Price

Chapter Seventeen

FIVE FOR ALL FOREVER

I t was there, written in the book plain as day. *Restorerbus Elemotis.* Or, in simple terms, the Lilies to Roses spell. Lilies, Willow figured, because they represented death, and roses because of the red bloom of life.

Ingredients:

Wisp Essence
Ent Root
Witch's spit (that one shouldn't be too hard to come by)
A rose grown under a harvest moon
A sampling of the thing you love most

"Of course, it's always the thing you love most," she quipped. "Typical."

Even if she could find ent root and wisp essence, Willow knew better than to use black magic to restore Montgomery to full life. And even if the spell did bring *some* dead people back to life, there was no guarantee it would work in Montgomery's unique situation.

Still, the temptation was rather alluring.

She ever thought it was possible to fall so fast—and so hard, too. And just her luck to find a soul mate who is more soul than man.

She'd called Esme last night after feeding Montgomery a good dinner and putting him to bed. Esme said she'd ask Gladys if she had any new information, but it didn't look good. For all intents and purposes, Montgomery could have been the first ghost in history to come back to life—sort of.

There really was no protocol for this.

Willow bit her bottom lip and turned the page. There were always warnings about using magic like this. Consequences. She was reminded of The Monkey's Paw—a book she'd read once about an elderly couple who were granted three wishes, but the wishes came with an enormous price. What price would she have to pay to give Montgomery life again?

If it was anything like the book, she didn't want it. Besides, she was vehemently against the cutting off of paws.

As if he could read her mind, Zephyr pounced on her lap and purred, expecting ear scratches.

"I think you're the thing I love most," Willow said, petting him. "But Monty might be stiff competition. No pun intended."

She decided not to open the shop that day since the whole town was getting ready for the Harvest Festival and wouldn't be buying books. It would give her some extra time to come up with a plan. The purple box hadn't moved since last night—to her knowledge. It might be on top of the roof for all she knew. She was too afraid to look inside the cabinet.

"Have you found anything yet?" Montgomery entered the room still in the striped pajamas she'd bought him. He was barefoot and unkempt with hair sticking out in all directions. And his mustache was poking up. The sight of him did something funny in her heart, and her tummy flip flopped in response.

She reaaally wanted to keep him forever and ever. If only there was a spell that wouldn't rain down hellfire upon her.

Closing the book with a satisfying thud, she said, "Not

yet. But I made a pot of tea. How are you feeling this morning?"

He yawned, stretching back his shoulders while scratching his chest. He might as well have been a cat.

"Rested," he said. "I think some sleep was all I needed."

Willow knew he was just saying that to ease her worry. She needed to do something and quickly. Something without Monkey's Paw results.

Montgomery sat at one of the bistro tables while Willow poured him a cup of tea from her silver teapot and served him a plate of warm cream cheese and butterscotch danishes. How domestic this all felt, like a scene from an old-fashioned movie and she wasn't even mad about it.

Montgomery seemed to think so too, because after the tea was poured and Willow's hands weren't otherwise occupied, he pulled her onto his lap and devoured her mouth like she was the first course in a very large meal. She was beginning to love the feel of his mustache against her lip so much, she'd sometimes absently tickle her face with the ends of her own hair whenever she'd think of him. It wasn't as good as the real thing, though and she hoped he would never shave it off.

She felt a deep moan coming from his chest before she heard it with her ears, and without even noticing she'd done it, moaned back with abandon. She liked this. She could get used to this. And considered for a moment to always keep the shop closed until at least eleven in the morning from now on. They could get a lot of kissing in before eleven.

In the haze and passion of the beautiful, lazy morning make out session, Willow vaguely heard her name coming from somewhere that wasn't Montgomery's lips. And unless he was a ventriloquist, and suddenly took on the voice of her mother, she concluded that they were being watched.

Esme cleared her throat and said, "Hello, excuse me. Sorry to interrupt."

Montgomery broke away from the kiss, heated and flushed a little, and turning toward the sound of Esme's voice said, "Can she see us?"

"I'm afraid so," answered Willow, and glared at the shiny silver teapot where Esme's face glimmered.

Getting off Montgomery's lap and taking her own chair, Willow adjusted her faded candy corn sweatshirt and glowered.

"Mother! Please use the phone I gave you. It has facetime."

She didn't add that she wouldn't have to answer if she didn't want to—unlike with mirror charms. She made a mental note to only use the clay teapots from now on.

"I did try using the phone, Willow. But you didn't answer it."

How convenient she'd left it upstairs, then. Except for the unfortunate shine on her silver teapot allowing her mother to communicate through it.

"Well you have me now. We were just having breakfast."

"I can see that."

Willow and Montgomery exchanged a flushed expression, and Willow realized how bad it might have looked from her mother's perspective.

Was she getting hot and heavy with the resident ghost? Yes. Yes, she was.

Nevertheless, she decided it was best to put that aside for now and focus on the bigger picture which was fixing whatever it was that needed fixing.

"Do... you have news from Gladys? Is there anything she can do for Monty?"

"I do have news, but it's not that. Sorry. What I'm about to tell you is of grave importance. It could mean life or death for more than one person. Otherwise, I wouldn't have... disturbed you."

Willow and Montgomery watched the teapot with a foreboding feeling and sat in rapt attention.

"It took Gladys a while to dig through all of it as this isn't just something any old witch can figure out. But she says she's certain what she found out is true."

Esme took a breath and steepled her fingers.

"Can we skip the dramatic pause please? I'm on pins and needles."

"You're aware—and I'm explaining it for Montgomery's sake as well—that there are many places around the world where ley lines converge. It's not entirely uncommon, but where they intersect, there's always a surge of magic where witches and wizard kind can go to renew their magical energy. Those places are particularly popular when there's a full moon, or during one of the solstices."

"And Gladys thinks Mysthaven is one of those places?"

"Yes but let me finish."

She took another dramatic pause, sending Willow's patience out the window.

"According to myth and legend, there is a Nexus with a high concentration of magical energy. It is said to be the source of all magic on the earth which travels to every living—or possibly dead—being on the planet. Any spell cast in the Nexus would be hundreds of times more powerful than anywhere else on the earth. Some believe it's located in Egypt or near the Mayan pyramids. But after thousands of expeditions, nobody has been able to find it. Until now."

Willow glanced at Montgomery to see if he was following this, but by the look on his face, she understood he was following just fine.

"You're telling me," Willow said slowly, "That Mysthaven Connecticut, a tiny town with only one gas station, is the most powerful place on the planet and nobody noticed?"

Esme shrugged. "The Daughters of the Twilight Veil noticed."

"Just splendid," said Willow sarcastically.

"And according to Gladys, there are possibly five Nexus

locations all working together like points of a star. Not just one. But she hasn't worked that out yet."

"How big is a Nexus. Is it as big as a town?" Montgomery asked.

"No. It's probably no more than one hundred feet in diameter, but the middle is where all the magic is concentrated. But here's where it gets interesting. I contacted a cousin of mine to see if she knew anything about our great aunt Celeste and, after chatting a bit, she remembered she had a few things in her attic collecting dust for decades. She found this in a box."

Esme displayed a small, aged book. It was bound in what looked like leather and wrapped with twine.

"It's Celeste's diary. She didn't write a lot of things in it. Mostly drawings of nature, recipes for harmless potions, what phase the moon was at any particular time, and what she had for lunch. But this one entry from February of 1912 is quite telling."

She cleared her throat and lifted the book near her nose to read it.

"Here's what she wrote.

'The sisters dance under the moonlight to charge their energy as they have done for centuries, so I'm told. I, being young and inexperienced, was surprised and delighted to have been invited to join them, and they have welcomed me with warm regard. There is a special magic here, one which has given the sisters power and youth beyond compare. In their wanderings they found it and return when the third full moon

coincides with perigee and passes through Earth's shadow. It is then that they come into their full power.'"

Montgomery's brow lurched down. "What does that mean? Perigee?"

Esme explained. "A perigee syzygy is when a full moon is close to the earth's orbit, making it appear larger than normal. We call it a supermoon these days, but that is not so rare as when it's combined with a blue moon and lunar eclipse at the same time. You might hear it called a super blue blood moon and it is a rare celestial phenomenon which happens only once or twice a century. But... when it's coupled with a cross-quarter day like Samhain..."

Awareness dawned on Willow's features. "Tomorrow!" she said.

Esme nodded solemnly. "Tomorrow. And, apparently on October 31st, 1912."

"And we're sure there's a Nexus in Mysthaven?" Willow questioned, just to cover all the bases.

"Here," Esme said. "There's another entry a few days later.

'This land was protected by the sisterhood for many years until it was taken from them and turned into a place of ill repute.'

That would be the Moonstone Saloon, I imagine. She goes on to say,

'I have been honored with a great task, and I will do it to be fully inducted. I will do anything to please the sisterhood.'"

Willow snorted. "She was trying to fit in. Talk about *Mean Girls* witchy edition."

"'*We are coming upon our sacred holiday and if we fail to take back our land of old, we will perish.*'

Obviously, they didn't perish. But they didn't accomplish what they wanted."

Montgomery smoothed down his mustache with his thumb and middle finger. "Why do they need to own it, though? The diary says they'd been coming here before anything was built on it. They didn't own it then."

"No, but there are laws in the magical world. Claiming ownership of land and building a permanent structure gives the title bearer absolute, exclusionary rights. Anyone can visit, and even benefit from the energy of a magical place. But only the owner is truly able to wield any power of significance. So that tells me they not only want to charge their magic, they want to use the power of the Nexus to do something big and terrible."

Willow's stomach dropped. "Terrible like what?"

"All currents run from the Nexus. If I were to speculate, whatever they have in mind, it will be detrimental to any other beings living along the ley lines."

"Why would they do that?" Montgomery cried. "Don't they have enough power? Why hurt innocent people?"

"Malice probably. Revenge. And you have to understand that it's not natural for a witch to live as long as they have. Their morals have gotten a little twisty over time."

Montgomery nodded knowingly. "Like Gollum."

"He finished the *Lord of the Rings* books," Willow said to Esme, resisting an eye roll. "Now *everything* is the hero's journey with him."

"Well then," said Esme. "We should form a fellowship, shouldn't we? There are five of them and only four of us—unless you'll join us, Montgomery."

Montgomery raised a brow in surprise and looked from Esme to Willow and back again. "But... I'm not magical."

And Esme laughed, shaking her head at him like one does to a child. "My dear man," she said. "Everything you're made of is magic."

"WITCHES EXIST
THROUGHOUT SPACE AND TIME."

—Amanda Yates Garcia

Chapter Eighteen

THIS IS HALLOWEEN

I t was a nice day as Wednesdays go. Not a cloud in the sky. Crisp, autumn air with a slight breeze that catches your hair in short, refreshing gusts. The laughter of children in the distance excitedly preparing to go out trick-or-treating.

Montgomery had heard the phrase 'it's a good day to die.' He couldn't remember where he heard it, but he thought it was completely ridiculous. It's never a good day to die. And if he was to die today for the second time, he'd be pretty bent out of shape about it.

However, he did accept the possibility he might meet his mortality once more against the same coven that did him in last time. If you did the math, the odds were high.

He put on a brave facade for Willow, though. Math wasn't his strong suit anyway.

Esme, Bliss, and Ivy arrived before breakfast and, since he was expecting them, changed out of his striped pajamas early, so as not to be caught indecent like the day before.

When he walked into the front of the shop, they were all drinking tea with Willow.

"Hello, mister," Bliss said amiably. "How's the mustache?"

"It's fine," said Willow. "Stop trying to convince him to let you glamour it up."

Truth be told, Montgomery wouldn't have minded a little help keeping his mustache in place. But Willow liked when it got all messed up. She told him as much last night.

"My mustache and I are ready," he said. Though exactly what they were ready for, he was not sure. He'd probably never be ready to fight evil witches, even with good witches at his side.

"We were just finalizing our plan for the day," said Willow. "Tea?"

"Yes please. And some of those apple tarts if you have them."

"I was just telling the girls," said Esme as Willow poured the tea, "that we should split up this morning when we cast protection spells on the town, that way we can cover more in less time."

Montgomery, not able to cast any spell, was eager to do something to help. "What would you like me to do?"

"You will sprinkle a barrier of salt. We brought enough to cover the entire perimeter of Mysthaven proper and a little extra for the town square, where the Harvest Festival will take place."

Ivy produced a bag of what seemed to be rocks and dropped it on the table with a soft clunk.

"I made these," she said, taking out one of the objects inside. It was a coin sized bead made of blue glass, painted to look like an eye. "We can hide them in places as we cast the protection charm around the square."

"These are beautiful," said Esme. "Truly stunning work."

Ivy seemed pleased with herself as he started passing the beads out to her sisters. "Thank you. They're made from copper, molten glass, iron, water, and salt."

"What are they?" Montgomery asked curiously.

"They are Nazar amulets," Ivy said. "And they're meant to shield people from evil."

Esme turned one of the beads over in her fingers. "An amulet is an ornament, really. Usually meant to wear like jewelry. They do have some protective qualities but aren't meant for big jobs."

"Big jobs like fighting the most powerful coven on the earth for instance?" Montgomery said cheekily. Willow passed him his cup of tea with a saucy glower.

"You're right about that," said Esme. "But for our purposes, the salt, the amulets, the protection spells... will be just enough to shield the town as we prevent the coven from even coming near it."

They'd sat down the night before, having a conference through mirrors, and worked out a plan. Willow had suggested they use a thing called Zoom. But the other witches wanted nothing to do with it. Especially Gladys, who was there as a sort of consultant. She was mostly useful, except for the ten or so minutes she went on about that time she got called up on stage at a Jimmy Buffet concert. Then she went off to magic up a margarita.

The plan was very simple. Not to let the coven get anywhere near the Moonstone. It would have to be carefully executed. Willow would go to the pre-festival gathering at Nadine Bickford's house. Meanwhile, the other Ravensong women would form a circle around the house, casting a spell (one of Gladys' special inventions), preventing anyone from leaving the house for at least twenty-four hours. The tricky part would be for Willow to sneak out before the spell took effect, but with just enough time so that the bad witches couldn't get out after her. Thus, keeping them away from the Moonstone and trick-

or-treating children while the super blue blood moon was in the sky.

Meanwhile, Montgomery's job was to lay down a long string of silver wire around Nadine's property. The silver would be inscribed with an incantation to drain power from magical beings. That was why the Ravensong witches could not do it themselves. Willow was worried the magic that was keeping Montgomery alive would seep out of him from touching the silver, but he seemed alright when he tested a small sample. Until then, the wire was stored in an iron box.

"Can you ride a bike?" Esme had asked Montgomery.

He replied that he could although it had been a while, but he quipped it would be just like riding a bike.

After breakfast, the team went about the town of Mysthaven planting the various protections against danger. The Ravensong women, already decked out in black robes and pointy hats, didn't draw the attention it would have on any other day. But on Halloween, it was not only encouraged but celebrated. In fact, people frequently muttered, 'nice costume' or 'looking good, ladies' and then there was the one guy who suggested they come over and stir his cauldron. Bliss gave the man a wart in the middle of his nose for that remark.

Montgomery had to admit, they did look rather stylish. With the robes flapping open as they walked, exposing shiny boots, long, stockinged legs, and taking strong, purposeful strides, they didn't look like anyone you'd want to mess with.

Montgomery simply sprinkled his salt everywhere the best he could.

They convened for lunch at Bo's ordering their steaks as rare as possible. It must have been a food witches ate when preparing for battle, Montgomery thought. Bo delivered the steaks medium and refused to cook them any less.

"You're not getting E. coli on my watch," he grumbled and walked away.

"What's with the town misanthrope?" Bliss asked.

Willow waved her hand down. "Oh, just a little local color."

"And what color would that be? Plaid?"

Willow shrugged, and was just about to cut into her steak, when her phone rang. She quickly took it out of her robe pocket and frowned.

"It's Astrid. Should I answer it?"

"Yes," said Esme. "If you don't, it might raise suspicion. They don't know you're onto them, do they?"

"No," Willow said. "I don't think so."

Montgomery placed a reassuring hand on her knee and that seemed to give her the courage to answer the call. She listened and nodded—not that the woman on the other end could see her nodding—and got in a couple of words in edgewise like, "Yes, I remember." And "I'll see you then."

When she hung up, she brought everyone up to speed.

"She just wants to make sure I didn't forget about our little get together at the Bickford house. They want me there at dusk." She signed. "I don't know what she has planned. "Why invite me over there when the Women's Business Council is supposed to be at the Harvest Festival in a few hours?"

She used the professional term in public for the coven. Less to explain to eavesdroppers.

Speaking of, Bo came by with a refill of Montgomery's soda just then. Montgomery drank a lot these days. He was always so thirsty.

Bo seemed to scoff when he set down the drink, and Willow was too curious not to ask, "Why do you do that?"

"Do what?"

"Make a little snorty sound whenever the Women's Business Council comes up in conversation?"

"It's nothing."

"No, it's not nothing. It's okay to tell me. I'm not friends with those old crones."

Bo laughed at that. "Old crones. That's one way to put it."

"So? You've lived here a long time. What can you tell me about them?"

"Bo looked around, and seeing he didn't have a lot of customers, blew out a hard breath and said, "My old man didn't get along with them. He'd say there was some-thing... off with them. But who cares, right? Bo Senior wasn't exactly a bowl of cherries, himself. But Nadine Bickford was always looking at my dad with the side eye, you know? He suspected there was something fishy going on with that law firm of hers. And he called her out on a couple of things. Nothing ever came of it. Anyway. I just don't like her. He was so upset one day after the Harvest Festival that he got in a big fight with Nadine. She and her friends didn't like the changes he was making. He wanted it more family-friendly and they said he was trying to promote some kind of agenda. I just remember he was so angry after that fight. A few days later, he had a heart attack."

"I'm so sorry," Esme said, and touched his arm in comfort.

"I'm not saying Nadine had anything to do with his death," Bo said. "Dad was a hothead and had high cholesterol. Just, sometimes I think he might still be here if he hadn't gotten into that argument. I dunno. Maybe he'd have gotten all bent out of shape over a leaky faucet or something and still would have had a heart attack."

"Sometimes you just need someone to blame," said Esme. "It helps with the grief."

"Yeah. I guess you're right." Bo sighed. "Sorry to ruin your lunch. The French fries are organic. No cholesterol here."

Montgomery wasn't familiar with the word cholesterol, but if it had anything to do with Bo Senior's heart condition, he had nothing to worry about, seeing as his heart wasn't even beating anyway.

"I'm sure they're as healthy as brussel sprouts," said Esme. "It was so nice to meet you, Bo. Thank you for sharing about your father."

Bo looked a little dazed but said, "Yeah. Brussel sprouts." Then he turned to walk away from the table, but stopped and pivoted saying, "You know. I don't usually spill my guts like that. I guess you guys are easy to talk to."

When he was gone and completely out of earshot, Willow said, "Okay, who did that?"

"Me." Ivy raised a single finger. "What? He wouldn't have talked otherwise. Now you know a little bit more about our adversary."

"She definitely put a hex on Bo Senior and made it look like natural causes," Bliss said.

"Are you sure you want to go into her house tonight?" Montgomery asked. "You don't need to go inside for our plan to work."

"I'll be fine," Willow reassured him. "Gladys sent this over with Esme."

She was wearing a silver chain with a teardrop garnet hanging at her breastbone. Montgomery had noticed it earlier thinking it brought out the natural hazel in her eyes. He didn't think it might be more than just a pretty stone, but Willow tapped it with her fingernails, and the garnet shimmered as if it was lit from within.

"It will shield me from harm."

"What I don't understand," Bliss said, "Is why meet at dusk? Isn't that the time the Harvest Festival starts?"

"My guess is they want plenty of time to fully initiate Willow into the coven before the moon is at peak illumination," Esme said. "Like they did with Celeste."

"I won't let that happen," Montgomery said. Then he wrapped a possessive arm around her shoulders. She didn't seem to mind it.

"SLEEP, THOSE LITTLE SLICES OF DEATH
— HOW I LOATHE THEM."

-Edgar Allan Poe

Chapter Nineteen

INTO THE WOODS

E sme stood in front of Montgomery and her three daughters like a drill sergeant.

"Broomsticks!" she cried.

The sisters echoed robustly, "Broomsticks!" And they held up their brooms, ready to go into battle. Willow was still feeling queasy about it. She was afraid of heights, she suddenly discovered.

"Bicycle!" Esme said next.

And Montgomery confirmed the bicycle was ready. "Bicycle."

"Do you have your silver wire?"

"In here." He patted the box in his arms.

"Good. And remember daughters. We are Ravensong witches. Even you, Monty. Tonight, you are an honorary Ravensong."

"Thank you."

Esme took a small sack out of her pocket and proceeded to sprinkle the contents along the front of the bookshop. It looked to be gold flakes from Montgomery's point of view, and as she let them fly from her fingers, they flittered up the walls before dissolving into the setting sun's rays.

"That will hold up until we get back," Esme said. "Zephyr. Hold the fort while we're gone."

Despite Willow's insistence that Zephyr was just an ordinary cat and nothing more, she could have sworn he winked at Esme with shimmering moxie.

"Montgomery, you are the most vulnerable tonight, so I'm going to cover you in a charm."

She waved her hand over him in a clockwise motion.

"Like a thorn to a rose

Let the whipping wind shield

As armor to your chest

Protection be sealed."

Montgomery, not used to the protocol of having a charm put over him, bowed chivalrously and moved to the bicycle to get going. With the box of silver wire still in his hands, he went to place it in the bicycle's wicker basket, but he had to shift something out of the way first.

Willow felt her whole face, neck, and chest burn with the embarrassment, because when he picked up the object, both her sisters hooted into peals of laughter.

"Nice book," said Esme. "Is that the recommended reading after Tolkien's works?"

Willow wanted to turn invisible. How could she forget the copy of *Ice Planet Barbarians* in her bicycle basket?

Montgomery wasn't bothered one bit. He simply lay the book flat in the basket and placed the box of silver wire on top.

But Willow noticed the tiniest crack at the corner of his mouth when he playfully caught her eyes with the briefest glance.

"Okay then," said Esme. "If you continue down this road, then veer right once you pass the bed and breakfast. We'll be right above you flying in formation. If you're not sure where you are, look up. Willow will take the lead."

"Me?" cried Willow.

Esme gave her that mom look and bade Montgomery to go.

The four women went around to the back of the Moonstone just in case there were curious people about who'd see them lift off into the sky on broomsticks. Nowadays, nobody looked twice at that sort of thing, what with illusionists making TikToks all over the place. But Esme didn't want to take any chances on this important night.

The last thing they'd need is local law enforcement forcing them to produce a permit.

"We have to be absolutely careful," Esme said. "We can't fail at the Bickford mansion. Under no circumstances can we allow the Daughters of the Twilight Veil to make it to the Moonstone. They have had a century to prepare for this night. We have had one day. Do you all understand this?"

The three sisters all nodded solemnly.

"And Willow. The Nexus has been growing in potency this past month. I need you to come to terms that when it goes back into a dormant phase, Montgomery may have to leave. I hate to say it or even think about it, but I also want you to be prepared. Guard your heart starting now."

Willow cast her eyes down, perfectly aware this was coming. She had been trying to prepare herself, but still hung on to hope. Even now, as she was in anticipatory grief, she wasn't willing to let go.

Esme held out her hand, prompting Bliss, then Ivy, then Willow to hold on to it. And as they clung to each other, a wave of the purest magic washed over them.

Without a word, Bliss and Ivy mounted their brooms, hovering while they waited for Willow. But Willow stared at her broom, suddenly frozen with fear.

"Remember what I told you, Pumpkin," said Esme cupping her palm over where Willow had a death grip on her broomstick. "Give yourself grace, and control your feelings. "You are not me. You are not your sisters. And you certainly aren't your great great aunt Celeste. You're

Willow Ravensong. So call upon Willow Ravensong's magic. You will only soar when you can just be yourself."

With that Esme hopped on her broom and waited expectantly for Willow to follow suit. There was no coddling, no giving her a little push. It was just time.

So, embracing her courage, Willow squeezed her eyes shut and wobbled onto her broom, flopping around about three feet above ground for a while. And then, once she felt steady enough—and not afraid to fall the three feet if she did flub it up—she opened her eyes. But she was much more than three feet off the ground. She was soaring above rooftops, wind in her hair, and with her mother and sisters at her side. She realized something. The unknown was a lot more frightening than flight.

Esme smiled proudly and led her daughters to file into formation with Montgomery below.

Willow felt her heart swell with something infinitely more powerful than the crippling fear she let thwart her magic all these years. She felt joy.

Everyone she loved in the whole world, and they were helping her without question. Her mother. Her sisters. And Montgomery, the old timer, pedaling down the road, sitting erect on the bicycle like Buster Keaton riding a dandy horse in one of those silent movies. As Willow glanced down on him, a little more of that happy feeling came over her. Even as the night spread out before them, as dangerous it might be, she would cherish this feeling for the rest of her days.

They arrived at the Bickford Mansion just before the

golden warmth in the sky faded into the hazy purple and blues of twilight. The moon hung low and large on the horizon, dark and red. Not quite ready for its performance. Willow wasn't sure if she was ready either, but here she was.

The others held back out of sight for the time being, and Willow, handing her broom to Bliss, marched right up to the front door and knocked.

She waited; heart lodged in her throat. Knocked again. Waited again. Then rang the doorbell. It was one of those big, gonging doorbells you'd find in haunted houses. A month ago, that would have scared her. But she didn't mind a little haunting anymore. Ghosts were people, too after all.

When no one answered, she clutched her garnet and creaked open the door. It was dark and quiet other than the distant ticking of a grandfather clock. She creeped slowly down the long hallway she'd walked down on that first day, and called out nervously, "Hello?"

There was no answer.

Swallowing hard, she placed her hand on the door-knob leading into the sitting room where the meetings were held. She didn't know what she'd find beyond those heavy, wooden doors. If the witches were waiting inside, they were being awfully quiet. It was like a surprise party without the fun bits.

She turned the knob and slowly pushed open the door. The room was as dark as the rest of the house, and no one was there. At least, she didn't notice anyone there. Until she looked up.

There, suspended from the ceiling, trapped in a glowing bubble, was Talon. He was just sitting in there, criss cross applesauce.

Willow gasped at first, then when she got over the initial shock, peeled her fingers from the garnet amulet around her neck. She didn't even realize she was clutching it so hard until her fingers ached from straightening them out.

"Talon! What are you doing up there?"

"I'm grounded," he said matter-of-factly. "My mom found out I stole her grimoire."

"Does she always put you in a bubble when she grounds you?"

Willow thought it looked like a convenient place to put a toddler when they got into mischief. Sort of a witchy time out. But she wasn't a mom, so you must forgive her ignorance of child rearing.

"Pretty much," he said, shrugging. "It's getting a little small for me."

"You're twenty-one," Willow said. "I could be wrong, but aren't you a little old to get grounded?"

"I guess. Can you get me out of here?"

"I don't know. What spell did she use?"

"Capti Fundatus."

"Hmm. I don't think I'm familiar with that one," she said, trying to sound sophisticated instead of completely clueless in the ways of magic. "But I know someone who might."

"Well, I can wait. I have nothing better to do."

"Where is your mother and the other Twihards?"

"Twihards. Good one." He didn't even crack a smile. "They're in the Cinnamon Woods."

"What? Why?" She would have to send a warning somehow before Esme and her sisters surrounded the house with the spell. And before Montgomery laid down the wire.

"How am I supposed to know? I've been trapped in a bubble all day."

"If it's any consolation, you look like a goth version of Glinda the Good Witch of the North in there. Are you hungry?"

"Nah. I'm good."

"Okay. I'm going to go find my family and get you out of here. I'll be back soon."

Talon uncrossed his legs and flopped backwards, making the bubble warble and shimmer. "I won't hold my breath."

"Charming as always," Willow mumbled, leaving the room.

When she went outside, she waved the other four over and told them what she'd learned.

"Should we wait until they go back in the house?" Bliss asked.

"I don't think they're going back in there," said

Willow. "And we don't know how long they plan to be in the woods."

"She's right, Esme agreed. "We need to find out what they're doing in the woods before we decide what to do next."

"I'm pretty sure they're not making s'mores and singing kumbaya," Ivy said. "Bad old witches in the woods equals little children getting eaten."

Willow liked s'mores and decided to introduce them to Montgomery if they ever got out of this alive.

"Yeah, I'm with Ivy," said Bliss.

"Then you two stay behind," Willow said. "Esme and I will go check it out."

"I'll go too," Montgomery offered.

"You don't have to, you know," said Willow.

"I'm already dead. What can they possibly do to me?"

The three of them headed off toward the woods, and not fifteen seconds later, Bliss and Ivy catch up to them.

"We never said we didn't want to come," said Bliss, and nobody said anything after that.

As it turns out, sneaking up on anybody with crunchy leaves underfoot doesn't really work. Sneaking up on four-hundred-year-old witches is even more impossible. So Esme, being pretty clever, cast a small levitation under their feet. Willow thought it felt like walking on marshmallows, and now she was really craving s'mores.

They seemed to be walking for a long while, but it was probably just the effects of the levitation spell. It made you walk slower.

Then, they caught a glimpse of crimson robes through the trees, and they were illuminated by a purple light. Careful not to make a sound, Willow and her party snuck a little closer, and could just make out unintelligible gabble coming from the circle of witches. They had formed rock cairns which they each stood in front of, and the source of the purple light was on a larger rock on the ground, perfectly in the center.

It was the Hobby Lobby crystal ball. Of course it wasn't actually from Hobby Lobby. We already established that. But Hobby Lobby is easier to remember than Orb of Gorimaan.

"What are they doing?" whispered Ivy.

"They're priming themselves," Esme whispered back. "Probably to wield the magic of the Nexus. It's too much power for a human body to bear. It could kill them."

"Well maybe we should go ahead and let them blow up," said Bliss. And they all gave her a flat look. "Just saying."

"We have to continue with the same plan as before but do it out here in the woods," Esme decided. "I'll take the North, same as before. Girls, you know what to do."

They certainly did, although now they were more exposed. They concluded that flying up above the trees was their best bet. Ivy to the East, Bliss to the West, Esme to the North, and Willow to the South. Montgomery would continue to walk on the marshmallows, wrapping the silver wire around trees.

When they were all in place, Esme started the chant, soon after joined by her daughters.

"Obligamus vos omnes ad hunc locum sic non excedere donec sol oriatur tertio die et cum exeatis longe ibitis."

They repeated it over and over until their words connected them at the four points with a surge of blue light. Willow was amazed and overwhelmed. Surely this kind of magic was too great for her. When she began to falter, Esme sent her one of those mom looks but telepathically since she was a ways away. She didn't know if she could hold up her end. She didn't want to be the weakest link. But then she glanced down and saw Montgomery fearlessly wrapping wire from tree to tree, and at that moment, she wanted nothing more than to be brave. So, she metaphorically pulled up her big girl panties, and focused on the incantation.

"Obligamus vos omnes ad hunc locum sic non excedere donec sol oriatur tertio die et cum exeatis longe ibitis."

The thing about a big 'ol blue square light in the sky, is that it will draw attention to those down below. And if those down below are up to no good, they won't take kindly to an opposing coven of witches trying to cast a spell on them.

But they didn't have brooms of their own so they couldn't very well fly up to stop the spell casting. But they did yell up at them. Most of what they yelled were curses and such, which won't be repeated here.

Nadine swooshed her arms around maniacally, channeling the purple essence of the Hobby Lobby ball, and flinging it upwards.

"You missed," hollered Willow, and that just made Nadine madder.

"If you're doing what I think you're doing," cried Nadine. "It will never work. You're one of us."

"What?" Willow shouted. "I can't hear you."

She could, in fact, hear perfectly fine.

Astrid covered the Hobby Lobby ball with her body as if it had to be protected at all costs. Daria and Rowena joined Nadine in swishing their arms about to fight off the Ravensong women, while Jewels... well Willow wasn't sure exactly what Jewels was doing other than running in a circle barefoot.

"Hold it, girls," Esme cried and surged her energy into the blue light until Willow, Bliss, and Ivy could feel it jolt through them.

All the efforts of Nadine and her coven turned out to be completely fruitless, being the ones down below. And even though they combined their forces to try to get at the Ravensong women, they seemed to be just out of reach. Or perhaps the trapping spell was working.

The Twilight coven went berserk, doing everything they could think of, it seemed. But then, Nadine stopped completely and instructed her sisters to do the same. She was looking at something just beyond in the wood, and Willow could hear a menacing laugh down below.

"Montgomery!" He was down there and alone.

Nadine thrust her arms out with a flash of light, sending a chord of purple energy coming from her fingers. And like she was pulling on a rope in a game of tug-of-war, lassoed Montgomery into the clearing where she and the other witches were doing their witchy ritual.

Willow flinched, reacting to the instinct to save Montgomery. But Esme held on to her with the channel of blue energy.

"We almost have them, Willow. Don't break it."

"Yes, but at what cost?" Willow cried. "They'll kill him."

"He's already dead. Stay the course."

But Willow's heart spoke louder than her reason, and letting go of the trapping spell, swooped downward, hoping the square would form into a triangle just long enough for her to rescue Montgomery from Nadine's magical purple lasso.

"Well, well, well, how adorable" Nadine said with a cackle. Came down to rescue your boyfriend, have you?"

She tugged tighter on the lasso, squeezing Montgomery's arms to his sides.

"Let him go," Willow demanded.

"Pledge your soul to us and I will."

Willow snorted. "You're such a cliche, do you know that?"

"You can't save him. Nothing you do will ever save him." Then she fixed her eyes on Montgomery and bared her teeth. "Isn't that right? Montgomery Harland."

Willow cast around. The other witches were trained on her, ready to strike.

"Did you think we wouldn't notice?" Nadine said. "How very typical of you, tending bar in the same fashion over a century after your death. What I want to know is how."

"It doesn't matter," Willow said. "We know your secret."

"And I'm happy you do because you could be so much more with us. Be one with us... your sisters."

"I have sisters."

"Or did you forget about us?" Ivy zoomed her broomstick through the clearing as if it was a hot rod. She threw down a red smoke, momentarily distracting the coven. Meanwhile, Bliss made her own magic lightning lasso. It was pink, of course. She weaved in and out of the clearing, threading like a ribbon. Meanwhile, Esme hovered above them all, twirled her finger once or twice, then seconds later, the bicycle came zipping through the wood until it found its place under Montgomery's derriere. Nadine lost her hold on him, and like a tidal wave carrying a daredevil surfer in a tropical storm, lifted Montgomery and the bike off the ground.

"Just hold on," Esme hollered. "The bike will do the driving."

"I certainly hope so," said Montgomery, gripping for dear life—even if that is a ridiculous turn of phrase for a dead guy.

But Nadine wasn't to be defeated that easily. With her eyes on Montgomery, she drew energy from the Hobby Lobby ball and formed it in her hands. Her intention was clear—to send it in Montgomery's direction. Willow cried out to warn him, hoping he was good at dodgeball.

And Montgomery, quick with reflexes and strong with his pitching arm, picked up the only thing within reach (which was *Ice Planet Barbarians*, naturally), and threw the book straight down on Nadine's face.

It hit her between the brows with a *thwunk*, and as she was momentarily stunned, Bliss tied off her magical rope thing, trapping the Daughters of the Twilight Veil in pink sparkles and glitter.

Their twisted faces could be seen from where Willow and company flew up into the sky until they were hidden behind the trees of the thick, Cinnamon Woods.

The flight back to the Moonstone carried the party on a triumphant wind, and all the Ravensong witches felt a victorious lightness in their hearts. They flew side by side in a line of five across. Montgomery seemed to take flying on the bicycle as naturally as riding it on the street, pedaling as if that was helping to keep him in the air—E.T. style. Willow smiled with her whole soul and decided she loved flying next to Montgomery on the bike, as long as he didn't have it in his head to phone home to catch a ride on a spaceship.

The moon rose higher in the sky, and as they flew into the town, a heavy fog was rolling in behind them. They did a quick sweep of the town square and were pleased to find the families having a good time at the Harvest Festival. Little ghouls and witches running amok with sticky faces and bucket loads of candy, while princesses and superheroes played carnival games and ate caramel apples.

Willow was proud of their efforts in protecting the town. Even Zephyr seemed proud of them by the way he meowed when they walked in the bookshop. But before they could break out the champagne, Esme gathered everyone around her.

"The trapping spell was incomplete but will buy us some time. How long before they find a way out of your... what exactly do you call that thing you did, Bliss?"

"I call it a Barbie Bind," Bliss said proudly.

"Interesting," Esme said. "How long will the Barbie Bind last?"

"I'm not sure. I've never used it on horrible witches before. Maybe an hour?"

"And Montgomery? How far did you get with the silver wire?"

Montgomery shook his head. "I would say I made it

roughly three quarters of the way around the trees surrounding them. But I placed it low, so maybe they won't see it in the dark and then trip on it."

"We can hope," said Esme. "They're clever and cunning. Do you have enough left over to surround the Moonstone? It might keep them out for a while."

"I... dropped it in the woods," Montgomery admitted. "When Nadine picked me up with that force."

"It's okay," said Willow. We have other protections."

"We can't just wait here like sitting ducks," Montgomery said. "Could we find more silver? We can go back and—"

"No," Esme said. "We're stronger here. On the Nexus."

"Yes," said Ivy. "But so are they."

"But you're forgetting one thing. Montgomery is the original owner. As long as he lives, Willow's claim to the property is null and void."

"Do you think that will work?" Bliss questioned.

"If it's one thing Astrid loves," said Willow, "It's bureaucratic loopholes. As long as she believes it, we have the upper hand."

"And they can't harness the power for themselves," added Bliss.

"That's right," Esme said. "But Montgomery can."

"FoR IN THAT SLEEP oF DEATH
WHAT DREAMS MAY COME,
WHEN WE HAVE
SHUFFLED oFF THIS MORTAL COIL."

-William Shakespeare

Chapter Twenty

SHOWDOWN AT
THE MOONSTONE CORRAL

They came at the witching hour, because of course they'd do something dramatic like that.

The first phase was to defeat them before they could step foot inside. Esme Bliss and Ivy would see to that. If they can't keep them out, Willow and Montgomery would be inside with a replica of the original deed to the property, owned by one Montgomery Harland. It was a fake conjured up by Esme, but the twilight coven didn't have to know that.

The four of them cast a protection on the perimeter of the Moonstone. It was as good as any magical 'keep out' sign, but shortly after midnight, a light rain began to fall. And everybody knows rain makes for terrible shielding spell conditions.

Still, they were all in place, ready for any tricks the bad witches might come up with.

It was not just after three in the morning, and Willow peered out the front window where Esme and her sisters stood guard. Every few minutes they'd take turns going round to the back alley.

"I know this doesn't mean much coming from me," Montgomery said to Willow, stroking the hair from her neck and kissing her behind the ear. "But I was proud of you today."

Willow sighed, rolling her head to the side to give him better access.

"It means the world, coming from you," she replied, a little breathy. If he kept at this, she'd be a puddle on the floor and then they'd find out just how useful she really was.

She turned in his arms and gave him her mouth and...

Tap, tap, tap.

Esme scowled at them from the other side of the widow.

"I can see you guys in there you know."

She made a gesture to shoo them away from the

window. "Stay in the back of the shop. When they come, I want you hidden."

Willow did as she was told, casting a little extra protection over the windowsills.

"I'm going upstairs to your apartment to check the lock on the window," Montgomery said. "I'll be right back. I promise."

He kissed her long and demanding, as men do in the movies when they're about to go off to war or on one of those wilderness survival trips. There's always that one guy who breaks a leg or cheats, ruining the whole camping experience for the others.

Willow didn't care for those shows.

She clutched her garnet, listening for his footsteps on the stair. He'd only been thirty seconds (she counted) when she sensed something behind her.

Spinning around, she found the Hobby Lobby crystal ball on top of one of the small end tables. It certainly hadn't been there before.

"Monty..." she called, not taking her eyes off of it. "Monty... hurry!"

She realized briefly there was little Montgomery could do against a menacing crystal ball, but she just felt safer with him near. He could also make himself useful by alerting Esme for her.

Then smoke started to come out of the thing. Big, pillowy clouds of smoke. And from the smoke, arose a looming figure. Then the figure split off into three. Then five. And as the smoke cleared, there stood the Daughters of the Twilight Veil.

It was a pretty good trick; she'd give them that.

The five witches seemed rather pleased with themselves, and each had a wicked smile spread across their features.

From the corner of her eye, Willow saw Esme through the front window, rushing toward the door. But before Esme could reach it, Nadine flicked her wrist, locking down the shop from the inside, dropping the blinds, and turning them from canvas to a heavy, impenetrable steel.

"Did you think you could stop us with your birthday party magic?" Nadine sneered.

"I don't care for pink," said Daria. "It got in my hair."

Rowena scowled. "Nice try blocking us in the woods. The silver didn't work."

"Face it," Jewels added. "You're no match for us."

"It doesn't matter." Astrid stepped forward. "She's a Daughter of the Veil. She can't remove the bracelet. The power of the Nexus belongs to our coven now."

"No it doesn't." Montgomery joined Willow and tucked her into his side. "It belongs to me."

He produced the deed, with his name written in big, scrawling letters. It was Bliss' idea to make it look aged and falling apart.

Astrid shot a flame from her fingers, but the document was covered in magic to give the impression it couldn't be contested. He was the owner. Not Willow.

"My contract of ownership is no good anymore," Willow said. "You've lost."

"You're dead," Nadine sneered at Montgomery.

"Do I look dead to you?"

Nadine and Astrid exchanged knowing mean girl looks —but with some kind of special witchy telepathy.

"Obviously Celeste couldn't deliver," Nadine said. "But Willow can."

"Oh yes," said Astrid.

And both women raised their arms, conjuring a rushing wind inside the bookshop, sending pages of the books all over. Willow felt a force lifting her off the ground, and the more she struggled, the stronger the hold on her. It was as if there were invisible ropes tied around her. And when she looked down, not only was her garnet on the floor several feet below her, but she was also wearing an old-fashioned wedding dress. The kind with too much lace.

"Willow!" Montgomery stretched out his arm to her, but she was just out of reach. Then he started to rise off the floor too, and his clothing transformed into a bad 70s tuxedo. They were both suspended in the air, completely helpless.

Willow tried to call out, but her mouth clamped shut with a sort of gooey putty, muffling her screams.

"What my dear?" Daria said. "Wedding day jitters?"

"You can't to thi—" Montgomery's mouth clamped shut with the same goo before he could finish.

"Excuse the wedding clothes," Jewels said. "We had such short notice."

With a malevolent grin, Nadine assumed the role of officiant and signaled Rowena and Jewels to act as witnesses.

From out of nowhere, an eerie, off key wedding march sounded, and Willow noticed a snake-like ring on her finger.

"Let's get this over with, shall we?" Nadine said with an oily sneer. "Do you Willow Ravensong, take this man as your lawful wedded husband? Of course you do."

She snapped her fingers, and Jewels levitated up to Willow, wrapped her fingers around her head and shook it up and down.

"She says yes," chirped Jewels.

"And do you, Montgomery Harland, take this woman... blah blah blah."

Jewels clutched Montgomery's head like a football and forced a nod out of him, too.

"Okay, that's that. You already have the ring. Then by the authority invested in me, I now pronounce—"

Just then, plaster crumbled down from the ceiling, followed by the roof caving in. And through it, Esme, Bliss, and Ivy crashed into the bookshop.

Willow cried tears of relief. Not because she didn't have to marry Montgomery. She might like to do just that one day... but pick out her own dress, among other things.

Esme extended both her hands out, wielding the wind inside the shop to her advantage.

"Nobody puts Baby in the corner!" she bellowed, and then Willow and Montgomery's invisible shackles fell off and they drifted down to the floor.

But Nadine shouted at the top of her lungs, "Man and wife!" And cackling, she wailed, "You're too late."

Now, this part reminded Willow of every wicked witch in every movie she'd seen, because Nadine swooshed around her arms, conjuring the wind to circle around her, and gradually, the floor opened up into vast nothingness.

That was definitely going to be expensive to fix.

"These are original hardwood," she shrieked. But the other witches in the coven were already in a magic match with Ivy and Bliss.

One of Ivy's talents was numbing her opponent. With a twitch of her elegant fingers, Rowena and Daria slumped to the floor unable to use their limbs.

"That should hold you for a hot minute," Ivy gloated, just as Jewels sent some kind of spell her way, which was quickly blocked by Bliss.

Meanwhile Esme and Astrid were literally pulling each other's hair, having discovered they were matched too well in magic. Zephyr didn't approve of a cat fight if he wasn't invited, so he pounced on Astrid's back, clawing at her clothing.

"Fight all you want," Nadine cried with a cackle. The wind had gained momentum and seemed to be coming from the big hole in the floor now. And Nadine chanted something ominous and probably super evil. Then extending her hand to Willow said, "Come, coven sister. All the power of the universe is ours."

For some reason, after all the crap this coven had put her and her family through, and the forced wedding and the creepy crystal ball, that last thing Nadine said really set Willow off. It's like she just snapped, and with clenched fists and gritted teeth, she felt magic race from her toes to the top of her head. It was a surge of power, akin to being electrocuted but she was the source.

Everyone froze, staring at her in awe.

"Willow," Esme said with open astonishment. "Your eyes are on fire."

But Willow was fixed on Nadine. "I don't need another coven. I am a Ravensong witch."

Somewhere in the distance, barrels of thunder cracked the sound barrier.

"You cannot break the Circlet of Nebula. It's a dark and all-powerful bond."

"You know what's more powerful than your stupid bond? Love."

Love for her mother and her sisters and the true unbreakable bond she had with them. No enchanted bracelet could ever replace that.

Willow realized as the words were coming out of her mouth, that it was the cheesiest thing ever. The cheese was so Velveeta, she could hardly contain groaning at herself. But it was the truth. And the cheesiest thing of all... it worked. She held up her arm and the Circlet of Nebula dissolved into dust.

The complete look of shock on Nadine's face gratified Willow for about one-point-two seconds. Then, the hag tilted her head with mild surprise and admiration and began to slow clap.

A slow, menacing grin stretched across Nadine's leathery face, and she said, "I knew you were worth bringing into the sisterhood. I'm impressed. But there's one thing you may not realize. Sisters!"

She summoned the rest of her coven to join her, all of them coming to stand on the edge of that great big hole in the floor which was the opening to the Nexus. "Show her."

One by one, each witch exposed her arm, putting their veins on display. They glowed an unnatural purple.

With her arms outstretched, Nadine's own veins became visible, glowing in the same way.

"Go ahead," she urged, "Look at your arms."

Willow lifted her hands, bringing her forearms to her eye level, and like watercolor paint on wet paper, the veins in her arms appeared with the same purple glow. The look of horror in her eyes was question enough.

"Remember the papercut?" Daria said, wiggling her fingers. "We're blood sisters."

The papercut. When they made her read that silly agreement. The sneaky witches.

At this, Esme, Bliss, and Ivy flew to Willow's side, but Nadine was quicker, pricking her finger, and sending a single drop of blood into the Nexus. From there, the floor stretched, separating Willow from her family. They ran to be by her side, but with every step, the floor stretched even more. And when Esme lifted her arms, they seemed to be stuck in molasses. It was the same with Bliss and Ivy.

Willow looked down at her feet. They were on the edge of the Nexus opening. One misstep, and she'd fall in.

"Join us or die, Willow. It's your only choice."

Astrid stretched her arm over the Nexus and pricked her finger in the same way Nadine did. The three others did the same, each one standing on the precipice of the gaping gap in the floor. It seemed to go on forever with no bottom in sight.

The witches spread out around the Nexus, so they could just hold hands without stretching too much. Then they began to chant.

Something surged inside the Nexus, sending a whirling mass of air upwards, encircling everyone in the bookshop. The evil witches reveled in it, drawing upon its power.

But then something remarkable happened. Outside in the street, a continuous droning skirl pierced through the night, the dissonant and humming undertone resonating beneath the detached melody. Was that... *Eye of the Tiger*?

Nadine cried a shrill shriek, covering her ears. "What is that terrible noise?"

The other four witches likewise crouched in agony, clawing at the sides of their heads.

"Well I'll be," Willow muttered under her breath. Dale was right. Bagpipes really did work against evil.

And in a way, they did. But the power of the Nexus was

too strong, and Dale was already halfway down the street. He would probably upset a lot of neighbors soon.

Enraged, Nadine drew power among her coven sisters and together, they curled their magic around Montgomery, bringing him right to the edge of the Nexus.

"I didn't want to have to do this," Nadine said. "There is more power in numbers but if you won't cooperate, you will have to be no more."

Willow realized in that moment, the only reason the coven wanted her to join them willingly was because she was the primary holder of the Nexus. They needed her, and were willing to get rid of all she loved to take what they wanted. And if that meant sending her to her death so they could inherit the power, they would do it.

"He could be immortal, you know," Astrid hissed like a serpent. "We know he won't last in his current form. We could fix that."

"Imagine," Rowena added. "You, in your full power with your beloved at your side. You'd be unstoppable."

"Don't listen to them," Montgomery cried. "They're lying to you."

Daria cackled and twisted her wrists, pulling Montgomery backwards over the opening to the Nexus. He was at a forty-degree angle, only held there by magic and the balls of his shoes on the edge. Willow reached out and clamped her hands over his arms.

"You can have your happily ever after," Jewels said in a slightly softer tone than her coven sisters. "Just like your books."

Then Willow felt a growing strength from the Nexus, like it was feeding her intravenously, and she pulled with all her might bringing Montgomery into her embrace. But she felt the tug of the other witches' magic and she fought with every ounce of strength to hold onto him.

Montgomery looked into her eyes with a tender sorrow.

"Do you know what's more powerful than love?" he said softly. "Sacrifice."

And that, she thought, was not Velveeta at all.

He studied her eyes as though he would be asked to paint them from memory and seemed so at peace.

"You have to let me go," he bade.

"No," she said, fighting back tears. "I can't."

But Montgomery gave her a gentle kiss, giving himself to her completely.

"My soul was meant for your soul. We'll find each other again. In eternity. I'll wait for you, and we'll find each other."

"Don't you dare give up now, old man," Willow sobbed even as her grip began to slip. "There's another way."

"It's okay," he said. "You can let me go."

His eyes sparkled a magnificent green and with a look of understanding, he nodded. And she returned the gesture.

He kissed her again, this time with all the love, all the dignity and noble sacrifice, and Willow felt a piece of her heart go with him. With unbearable pain in her soul, she let her fingers slip, and watched him as he plummeted down, down, down, until he was gone in a brilliant, white light.

Everything inside her ripped down the middle and she screamed a primal, horrid cry. Tears poured out of her eyes, and out of that deep sadness, rage surged forward, and the torrent of the Nexus filled her.

Nadine and her coven cackled with glee, and said in unison, "Now you go to a horrible end. From dust you came, to dust we send."

But Willow was far too furious to waste time on their icky incantations and began to chant over and over, "Ego flexilis et lentum est. Quodcumque dixeris, resilit mihi et tibi haeret."

Nadine laughed and flexed her fingers to finish Willow off. But nothing happened. The power had drained from her. She tried again. Rowena tried to conjure something with her hands. Astrid flapped her arms about. But they had no magic.

And then, slowly and terribly, their beauty began to fade. Their skin became ashen with wrinkles growing deeper and deeper.

From their weakness, the spell holding Esme, Bliss, and Ivy dissolved, and the room snapped back into place. Clenching her fists, Willow crushed the crystal ball where it sat. With only a thought, burned the dark magic grimoire to a crisp, and waving her hand, sent them both into the hole in the floor. She then waved her arm, closing the Nexus, and advanced on her adversaries, continuing the chant.

Ego flexilis et lentum est.
Quodcumque dixeris, resilit mihi et tibi haeret.

Her sisters and mother came behind her, supporting her magic with their palms on her shoulders.

Ego flexilis et lentum est.
Quodcumque dixeris, resilit mihi et tibi haeret.

"What are we chanting?" Bliss whispered.

Esme replied quietly, "I think it means... I'm rubber and you're glue. Whatever you say bounces off me and sticks to you."

Then, illuminating from under Willow's skin, a glow both hot and cold at the same time, completely enveloped her until she was cloaked in light. And with fear and trembling, the Daughters of the Twilight Veil crumbled into dust.

"There are nights
when the wolves are silent
and only the moon howls."

-George Carlin

Chapter Twenty-one

THERE HE GOES AGAIN

Willow collapsed to the floor with exhaustion and her sisters flew to her side. They carried her away from the splintery wood floor to a spot where there was once a lush Persian carpet, but now was only a remnant. They laid her down with a few cushions that had been part of a comfortable chair. Now the chair was wedged in the wall along with a few side tables.

Esme brought Willow a glass of water, but changed her mind and turned it into a shot of espresso.

Willow couldn't bring herself to get up—not because her body wouldn't allow it—but because of the intense grief overwhelming her.

Montgomery was gone.

The first rays of sunlight filtered through the cracks in the iron clad windows. Bliss flicked a finger, changing the blinds back to a cream-colored canvas. She gave them a little more flair than before and added an off-white floral pattern you'd only be able to see if the light hit it just so.

Willow cast her eyes around her. The bookshop was a flipping mess. Books everywhere. Bar supplies in shambles. Somehow, that made her chuckle inside. It would drive Montgomery up the ever-loving wall.

The women remained silent for a long while, none of them wanting to voice what everyone was thinking. They didn't have to. Willow knew her mother and sisters were mournful on her behalf.

"Do you think he's still here?" Willow asked after thinking about it for close to an hour. "As a ghost?"

Esme unstuck a strand of hair from Willow's cheek. The tears had long dried but left behind a few crusty tracks.

"You saw him move on," she said. "He's at peace now."

Willow let out a hard breath. "I know. I just... was hoping."

She was hoping, yes. But at the same time, she felt it

was selfish of her, so she held the memories of him in her heart. Even the annoying ones.

"We need to get some food in you," Esme said. "What do you want us to conjure up?"

"Bliss makes the best strawberry cream cheese pancakes," Ivy said. "Unless you want pumpkin."

Willow sat up, realizing her sisters were probably famished, and squeezed their hands.

"Actually," she said. "I know a place."

Fifteen minutes later, piles of pancakes, eggs, bacon, sausage, and cinnamon buns were spread out before them at the biggest table they could find at Bo's Diner.

The Ravensong witches shoveled forkfuls of food into their mouths Henry the Eighth style. They were ravenous.

"Where do you girls put it all?" Bo asked with a slightly repulsed look on his face.

Monkey grunts were the only response. He rolled his eyes and held up the carafe. "More coffee?"

Without lifting their faces from their food, they all held their cups up high.

"I'll take that as a yes," he said and topped off their mugs.

Willow swallowed a big bite and said, "You need bigger mugs."

"I'll keep that in mind. Nice costumes, by the way. Looks like you had a wild night."

"You have no idea," Ivy said.

"I'm guessing you partied until dawn."

The women exchanged a brief knowing look.

"Something like that," Esme replied, and took a bite of sausage.

Bo cringed a little. "Remember how I said we don't serve cholesterol here? I lied."

"We're not worried about it," Bliss said. "Can you bring us some of those pink glazed donuts?"

"Yeah. Sure. Right on it," Bo grumbled, and stomped away, and the witches continued to inhale their breakfast for the next forty minutes.

"I guess we should get back to clean up the mess," Ivy said after they'd pretty much cleared the table.

"Yeah, agreed Bliss, rubbing her tummy. I'm beginning to regret that last donut. I feel like a balloon."

Willow gasped. "Oh no!"

"What? What is it?" Esme questioned.

"I forgot about Talon Bickford. He's still stuck in that bubble."

"Oops," said Bliss.

"I'm sure he's fine," Ivy said.

Esme squeezed Willow's hand. "I'll take care of it. And also break the news about his mother to him."

"That'll cheer him up," said Willow.

"He'd look so much better without that trucker hat," said Bliss absently.

"Who? Talon Bickford?"

"No, silly. Him." She nodded in Bo's direction.

"Don't even think about it," Ivy warned. "He'll notice if you put a glamour charm on him."

"Not if I do it gradually. He'll think it's all his idea."

Esme got up from the table and stretched. "I better get going. I'll meet you girls back at the Moonstone?"

Willow pulled her chair from the table but didn't feel like getting up just yet. Part of her wanted to poof the Moonstone off the planet, but that would be unfair to Montgomery's memory.

"Well, the bookshop isn't going to clean itself," she said with a sigh.

"We'll help you," Ivy said. "As soon as I can get Bliss out of here."

Meanwhile, Bliss was staring at Bo, wiggling her little finger. Suddenly, the fish on the front of his hat was gone and was replaced by a sailboat.

"Baby steps," she snickered, and held up her coffee mug for a refill.

Esme kissed her daughters and left the diner, and as Willow was leaving, Ivy promised they'd only be a few minutes behind her.

She slogged along the sidewalk, not entirely enthusiastic about going back to the Moonstone. The exterior showed no signs of a massive magic battle, but once she walked through the door, she'd be hit by a melancholy beyond words.

But upon entering the shop, there were no broken chairs or books stuck in the ceiling. There was no splintered wood or shattered glass. It was completely clean and restored back to its original condition. Actually, it was better. And Willow felt a pang in her gut. Esme must have done this on her way to the Bickford Mansion.

Filled with gratitude, she ventured further into the shop. How had her mother known the exact way she liked things arranged? All the tables and chairs were restored, the bar was in order, and all the bookshelves were put back with all the books set as before.

Then again, there was something new there. Stretching high from the floor to the tip of the highest of her bookcases was a sturdy wooden ladder hinged on a sliding rail. Willow approached it reverently, gliding her fingertips along the sides, noting the intricate carvings and embellishments.

"It's just what I wanted," she whispered to herself. And she held on to her heart lest she begin to cry again.

"Do you like it?"

The voice behind her was deep and smooth, like chocolate poured over silk. She closed her eyes, wishing he was not the ghost she bickered with, but the man she fell in love with.

"I love it," she said, and her voice was almost completely lost in a breath.

Gathering the courage, she turned to face him. Montgomery stood in the middle of the shop, looking every bit the handsome man she was head over heels for. But there was something... changed about him (other than his clothes—and thank the Fates that 70s tuxedo was gone). He was a little bit broader, a little bit tanner, and his skin had the healthy glow of a person who worked and lived and aged heartily to a robust thirty-one years.

And something else. His eyes were brown. A lovely, earthy shade of brown with a sprinkle of gold flecks in them.

"How?"

Montgomery closed the distance between them and produced a cloth handkerchief seemingly out of nowhere and dried her tears.

"Well, I had to look up what a *Beauty and the Beast* rolling ladder was, but then I figured it out from there."

Willow laughed through the tears. "Thank you. But I mean... how are you here?"

He smiled softly, dabbing her mascara with the handkerchief, then kissing each cheek.

"When I fell, there was no bottom, no dark abyss... not even cherubs playing harps. I was just existing, feeling nothing. But then, it was almost like my spirit shed off the skin and the bones... but it wasn't the same as when I died a century ago. It was more like how a butterfly sheds its cocoon. And before I knew it, I was standing here but you weren't. And I thought for a second that I was doomed to wander inside this shop—forever a ghost. But then, I felt it. My heartbeat."

Willow threw her arms around him and held on tight, unable to even comprehend this feeling of solace and elation.

Montgomery gathered her face in his strong hands and kissed her reverently. Willow sensed a familiar magic in his touch and knew in her spirit that Montgomery's new body was quite different than before. He was whole, and could only have been fashioned by the energy and magic of the Nexus.

"Wait a minute." She shook her head, trying to understand fully. She'd had a rough night with no sleep, and she probably wasn't thinking straight. "I was gone less than an hour. When we left here, it was in shambles."

Montgomery shrugged. "I looked around and thought to myself, 'what a dreadfully horrid mess' and then everything shifted into order as though by sheer will of thought."

"So, *you* did all this? With magic?"

"I don't really know what to call it," he said. "Not science, probably."

Willow had always known that being a witch was hereditary. One didn't just become a witch one day. Whatever magic Montgomery could now wield, it was much purer and potent than witchcraft.

"So..." Montgomery slid his hands down to her waist. "What do you want next? Mrs. Harland."

Willow liked the sound of that and moaned at the feeling of his hands on her.

"Regrettably, I don't think the wedding vows were valid," she said.

"You're still wearing the dress."

Right.

She groaned, thinking the tattered lacy thing made her

look more like the creepy beating heart bride at Disney World.

Montgomery traced his hands along her curves, caressing featherlight fingers up her spine, kissed her, and stepped back to admire his handiwork.

She looked down at herself and grinned. She was now wearing the pristinely white, free of green apple Schnapps stains, 1912 fashion gown she wore to the ball.

She gazed up at him lovingly and brushed her fingers over his mustache. "You're going to be impossible to live with, you know."

Montgomery pulled her close, rasping against her lips.

"Then you better get used to me," he growled. "Because I'm not going anywhere."

gigi's note

I hope you enjoyed reading Bewitching the Ghost. I had a blast spending time with Willow and Montgomery in their magical world. It was a fun departure from my non-magical romcoms.

If you loved what you read and want more laughs, banter, and sizzling kisses, visit gigiblume.com for more titles to swoon over.

acknowledgments

This book would really stink without help from the following individuals:

- Carina Taylor
- Kristyn Fortner
- My daughter Mia
- Samantha (Mia's friend)

A huge acknowledgement to my fellow Monster Mash authors: Ellie Hall, Ash Keller, Sophie-Leigh Robbins, Anne William, and Lindsey Jesionowski. This project has been loads of fun and I'm so happy to work with you.

Make sure you check out their books in the Monster Mash RomCom Madness Halloween event.

https://www.elliehallauthor.com/mashup

I also want to give special thanks and appreciation to the amazing bookstagrammers who have helped me celebrate this book and for their time and talent to give Bewitching the Ghost a moment in the light. They all have great content. I highly recommend you follow their accounts:

- _justagirlandherbooks
- Webreakforbooks
- thebookishbrunette_reads
- desert.diva.reads
- aprilsbooknook_
- lyon.brit.andthebookshelf
- hiding.in.the.pages
- storyhooked
- micahs.bookshelf
- misspippireads
- lindzanne1_bookworm
- modernmissgranger
- the.bookish.mom
- delightfullybooked
- thebookishdachshund
- _astoldbyem
- smalltownbookmom (Canada, is physical a possibility?)
- thesharpereader (Canada)
- __bookish.love__
- books.for.you.2
- abbys.always.reading

about the author

Gigi is a USA TODAY bestselling author and hopeless musical theatre nerd who has perfected the art of lolly-gagging.

Former professional wedding singer, Gigi lives in Southern California with her personal chef...er...husband and two weird and awesome teenagers.

When Gigi's not writing like a crazy woman, she likes to belt out showtunes, embarrass her kids, and spend all her free cash on books.

Printed in Great Britain
by Amazon